SEXY SUIT

A Cocky Hero Club Novel

J.H. CROIX

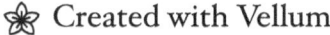

INTRODUCTION

Sexy Suit is a standalone story inspired by Vi Keeland and Penelope Ward's Stuck-Up Suit. It's published as part of the Cocky Hero Club world, a series of original works, written by various authors, and inspired by Keeland and Ward's *New York Times* bestselling series.

Chapter One

RYAN

My eye caught on the poster. *LOST DOG!!!!* The all caps words with four exclamation points were in bright blue font. I didn't know why, but I presumed the author of this poster would've added more exclamation points if there'd been enough space.

Stopping in front of it, I lifted my phone to snap a quick picture of the poster, immediately wondering why. On any given day, I passed plenty of announcements papered all over the place and ignored them. This was New York City, after all.

Yet, something about this poster snagged a tiny hook in my heart. The dog in question was an interesting looking dog. Barnable, as the poster labeled him, had the build of a

Corgi with a bread loaf sized body and sturdy little legs. However, unlike the typical ears that stood up on Corgis, this little guy had two ears that half-flopped down. He was mostly black with brown and white markings.

The woman in the photograph with her hand curled around the dog's leash was something else altogether. She had a mass of dark curls tumbling around her shoulders. Her skin was a creamy bronze. Even in this not very good photograph, her dark chocolate eyes popped out. She looked like a country girl misplaced in the city with her cowboy boots, denim jacket, and white eyelet skirt over a pair of tights.

I shook my head and kept on walking, telling myself I'd keep an eye out for the little dog. Minutes later, I settled into a seat on the subway and perused my emails as I zoomed from the Upper West Side to my office in downtown Manhattan. A short ride later, and I arrived at my office building, immediately throwing myself into my first meeting of the day.

Many hours later, during my final phone conference of the day, I stared at the phone on my desk, narrowing my eyes. "I don't think so," I said, my words clipped.

"Ryan, I'm sure—"

I cut the idiot off. "Oh, I'm sure. No deal."

At that, I tapped the button to end the call and stood from my desk, shaking my head as I did. There wasn't much I hated more than having my time wasted, and this fool had done just that.

I owned Talton Tech Industries. My grandfather started the company, well before the early days of computers. Things had changed quite a bit since he'd passed away, and I'd taken over the management. We navigated software, security, and the like. After I turned the company's fortunes around over the last few years, I found myself fielding requests with frequency to consider all kinds of funding for tech projects. This call hadn't been anything more than someone's pet project without a plan.

My eyes landed on the clock above my door as I turned to snag my suit jacket and walk out. The hands on the clock were barely a minute past 9:00 p.m. It didn't even faze me that I'd been in my office since before sunrise. I was a workaholic, and I didn't care.

———

"Come on, Barnable," a female voice called with a distinct southern twang.

Standing in front of my brownstone in the Upper West Side, I eyed the pair of cowboy boots sticking out from under my stairs. The sound of glass breaking reached my ears, and anger flashed through me. Stepping close to that pair of cowboy boots, I looked down and was greeted by the sight of a woman on her knees with a delectable bottom encased in denim.

What the hell was going on?

"Excuse me? Are you actually breaking into my house right here on the sidewalk?"

The woman let out a squeak. Her bottom shimmied as she scrambled back on her knees. Turning, she clambered to her feet, wincing and grabbing at one of her hands with the other. "Oh no! I think I cut myself."

"On the glass from breaking my basement window?" I asked dryly. I supposed I should've felt threatened, but there wasn't anything threatening about this woman. If she was a thief, she was remarkably terrible at it.

Her eyes whipped up to mine, and I was struck with a jolt of recognition. She was the woman from the missing dog poster. I'd noticed she was pretty in that grainy photograph. Up close and personal, pretty didn't even come close to capturing her. She was arresting.

Her eyes were wide as she peered up at me. Her dark hair glittered under the streetlights. I'd bet she had on the same cowboy boots I'd seen in that photograph. Her boots were paired with fitted jeans that hugged her curves and what I could only describe as one of those poet shirts. It was deep blue and swung around her hips loosely, teasing me with a hint of curves underneath.

"I wasn't trying to break in!" she blurted out.

"No? Then, why did you break the window under the stairs?"

"Okay, okay, I know it's going to sound crazy, but one side of it was already broken. I was just punching out a little more glass."

She said this so earnestly I couldn't help but believe her. That said, I tended to be skeptical. Habits die hard, and all that.

"Are you fucking kidding me?"

She shook her head wildly. "No! My dog is in there. I heard him barking. He must've gotten cold. Maybe he got in the basement through another way, but I heard him bark. Look under there. I swear I'm not lying," she said, gesturing toward the window under the stairs.

Against all common sense, I silently decided she might be telling the truth. I also happened to know my brownstone's basement connected to the one next door, and I'd spoken with the neighbors about getting their broken bulkhead repaired just last week.

It was then I noticed she was definitely injured. The trail of blood running down the side of her hand shone under the streetlights above. I didn't want her bleeding out here on the sidewalk. "Come in," I said, turning and striding up the stairs.

When I didn't hear footsteps behind me, I glanced over my shoulder and saw her waiting on the sidewalk.

"Barnable is down there," she explained.

A sharp bark reached me. I presumed Barnable was the dog from the poster I'd seen. "I'm well aware. But I'm not crawling through a broken window when I can get into my own basement by going inside and walking down the stairs."

"Oh!" She hurried up the stairs behind me. As I fit my key in the lock, she stood beside me, actually bouncing up and down on her heels.

The motion sensor lights came on the moment we stepped into the foyer. I couldn't have said why, but the moment I shut the door and glanced over at the woman with me, I became acutely aware of just how cold and impersonal my place was. Marble tile echoed under our footsteps.

I tossed my keys on a table by the door and turned to get a better look. "Let me see your hand."

"Can we check on Barnable first?"

"Your dog will be fine. I'd rather make sure the bleeding isn't too serious."

She let out a huff and then shrugged before holding her hand out. There were two deep gashes—one on the outer edge of her palm and another further up on the outside of her wrist. Both wounds were bleeding quite liberally.

"Just give me a paper towel. Let's go check on Barnable because he might be bleeding too," she said quickly.

"Mind telling me your name?" I replied wryly.

"Addie, Addie Castille," she said rather enthusiastically as she held out her bloody hand for me to shake.

I shook my head. "I'll pass on the handshake."

"What's your name?" she asked as I turned and began to stride down the hallway into the kitchen to fetch the requested paper towel.

"Ryan Blake," I called over my shoulder.

I was irritated—at the situation and at myself for having such a powerful reaction to this woman. Under the soft lights—atmospheric because that's what the decorator I'd hired had insisted on—Addie went from arresting to stunning. Her rich brown eyes stood out against her dark hair. Her southern twang set every cell in my body alight.

She was like a sunflower sprouting through a crack in the sidewalk in winter. She was *that* out of the ordinary. In my world, she was an utterly bracing breath of fresh air and absolutely, positively nothing like any woman I'd ever encountered.

Most people, when caught actually breaking a window into someone's home, might be worried at how it could be perceived. Not her. She was so certain it made sense to try to get her lost dog out of my basement that she wasn't worried I might call the police.

We walked into my kitchen, which felt even more echoing than the rest of my place. Tile floors, stainless steel appliances, and granite counters didn't lend any softness to the space. Addie was right behind me and stuck her hand out. My eyes landed on the tattoo curling around her wrist, with the gashes and blood running over it, I couldn't quite make out what it was. Black lines that curled sensuously before they disappeared behind the blood.

I handed her several paper towels. She snatched them and quickly wrapped them around her injured hand before asking, "Can we go into the basement now?"

Although I was concerned she needed stitches, I could tell she was probably going to find her way to my basement on her own if I tried to delay any longer. "Word of warning," I began as I turned away. "This brownstone has been updated within an inch of its life on every floor but the basement. It's a one hundred and fifty-year-old basement. It's dark, dank, and not the cleanest place. I can't even remember the last time I walked down there."

Undaunted, she simply nodded. "I grew up in New Orleans. I'm used to old buildings and haunted houses. As long as you don't lock me down there, I'll be fine."

I led her down the hallway to the laundry room where the entrance to the basement was. I was relieved the light actually worked in the basement stairwell.

The moment Addie called out on the steps, the very dog I'd seen on the posters in the area came barreling towards us across the stone floor. He was covered in dirt on one side, and he was beyond ecstatic to see Addie.

With blood seeping through the paper towels hastily wrapped around her hand, Addie knelt down on the floor and scooped the little dog up in her arms, talking a mile a minute. "Oh Barnable! I've been so worried. You got lost, and I thought I'd never find you!" Her hands stroked over his wiggling body. "You seem okay. Sweet boy, what happened? Are you cold? Are you hungry?"

As I watched their reunion from the foot of the stairs in my dim, dusty, dank basement, I marveled at the fact that my heart squeezed just a little at the amount of love Addie so clearly had for her dog.

Addie stood, bundling the little dog in her arms and looking over at me. "Do you know where the closest vet is?"

Chapter Two

ADDIE (ADELAIDE)

Sexy Suit—as I'd immediately dubbed the man the moment I got a good look at him inside the entrance to his rather sterile and cold brownstone—stared at me blankly.

"A veterinarian?" I prompted as I tried to keep a hold of Barnable in my arms while he wiggled madly and licked my chin.

Sexy Suit gave his head a little shake before replying, "There's one a few blocks away. Before the vet, we need to get your hand looked at."

"No." I tried to inject as much authority in my tone as I could muster. Everything this man said came out all stern and authoritative, like he just expected people to obey him.

"Barnable's got blood on his side. I'm afraid he's hurt."

Sexy Suit simply shook his head and turned to ascend the stairs. "Follow me."

Seeing as I didn't really want to hang out in the basement too much longer, I followed him. When we got upstairs, Barnable's wiggling proved too much for my hold. He slipped free, landing on the floor with an inglorious thump. Like a boat righting itself in the water, he bounced up and began licking the toes of my boots excitedly.

Sexy Suit kept on walking straight into the kitchen. I followed because I didn't know what else to do. Slipping his phone out of an inner pocket in his suit jacket, he tapped the screen and lifted the phone to his ear. "Mr. S–" I began, catching myself in the nick of time before I called him Mr. Sexy Suit to his face.

His sharp gaze met mine. "It's Ryan."

"Ryan, just tell me where the vet is, and I'll get out of your hair. Actually, I'll look it up," I said, fumbling for my own phone and belatedly realizing I didn't even have my purse on me.

Ryan ignored me. "Ryan here," he said to whoever answered on the other end of whatever phone call he was making. "Can you come take a look at an injury?" His eyes flicked to me, icy blue and inscrutable.

After another minute, he nodded. "Thank you. See you soon."

I eyed him. "I need to go to the vet."

Ryan looked down at Barnable and lifted his gaze to mine. "You're definitely bleeding more than him."

My belly did a full-blown tumbling routine the moment Ryan's eyes locked onto mine. It was all rather unsettling. Needing a distraction, I yanked my eyes free and looked down at Barnable. He was a little dirty, and there was something oily smeared on one shoulder.

Kneeling down, I ran my hand over his back. "Hey, buddy, what's going on over here?" I asked conversationally. When I reached the area on his shoulder where he had blood smeared, he paused in cleaning his chubby feet and looked up at me. "Does it hurt?"

"He's not likely to answer," Ryan said wryly.

Irritation zipped through me. I might've thought Ryan was, well, sexy, but he was also arrogant, cold, and not the least bit amusing. Flicking my eyes to him, I replied tartly, "Maybe not in words, but if he gets a little cranky, he's probably in pain. Obviously, you've never had a dog."

Returning my attention to Barnable, I was surprised to hear Ryan's reply. "I've had a dog."

I filed that little detail away. Sifting my fingers carefully through Barnable's wheat brown fur, I spread it apart to see a thin cut. The blood had already dried, and it didn't appear he would need stitches. I still wanted to get him checked out though.

Barnable emitted nothing more than a little sigh when I touched the cut lightly. Relief washed through me. Barnable had gone missing three days ago, a single day after he moved here to New York City with me. I'd hardly slept since he'd been gone and had been walking the unfamiliar streets by myself looking for him.

"He's probably okay," I said, glancing up to Ryan. "I'll still take him to the vet just to make sure it's clean and everything."

Ryan nodded, his eyes coasting over my face and down to my boots as I straightened. If I didn't know better—and I definitely knew better—I'd wonder if he was checking me out. But that's not how it felt. I knew I didn't quite fit in this pristinely clean kitchen with stainless steel appliances polished to a sheen, dark gray counters, and black and white tiles.

I took a moment to absorb the sight of Ryan. He wore a navy blue suit. Aside from me, that navy was the brightest speck of color in this room where everything was black, white, and silver. I imagined his shoes were quite expensive. His slacks were pressed, and he even had a vest on underneath his suit jacket. When my eyes reached his face, one side of his mouth kicked up at the corner.

"Are you quite done?"

I felt my cheeks heat, but I lifted my chin. "Yes. You're pretty uptight, you know?"

A dark brow rose in a slash, and haughty didn't even capture the look he gave me. "You were breaking into my house. Forgive me for being a little uptight about that."

I didn't know why, but this man, too damn sexy for his own good, set my entire body alight with sensations pinging through me.

He shrugged out of his suit jacket and hung it over the back of a stool beside the counter. As he turned, my eyes snagged on his broad shoulders, which filled out his shirt quite nicely. I'd have never thought a suit could turn me on, but on this man, it seemed indecent. His muscled shoulders shifted as he turned back to face me. When he rolled up his sleeves, my eyes got stuck on the subtle flex of his forearms.

Sweet Jesus. Apparently, I had a thing for forearms. I didn't even know forearms could be a *thing*. When my eyes swung up, I found him watching me watching him.

I squared my shoulders and lifted my chin. "Fine. Go ahead and call the police on me. Obviously, Barnable was cold and wet. I don't know how, but I guess he figured out how to get into your basement."

Ryan's eyes flicked to Barnable and back to me. "In these old buildings, many of the basements are connected. I'm pretty sure he got in through the neighbor's basement door, which was broken recently. I saw your posters, by the way."

"I hope so. I put them everywhere. I just moved to New York City three days ago. Barnable's never been here, and he got lost the first day we got here. I think he slipped out the back while I was unpacking some boxes. I was afraid I'd never see him again. It's crazy cold to him here since he's only ever lived in New Orleans. I'm sure he was just looking for somewhere warm. I heard him barking from the street." I paused, feeling a little ridiculous that I'd almost tried to crawl through a broken window to get to Barnable. "He's my only friend here, so..." I took a breath and shrugged. "I'm sorry about your window."

"You just moved here three days ago?"

"Yes."

That glacial gaze swept up and down me again before holding fast on my face. "That explains your Southern accent."

"Being born and raised in New Orleans definitely explains my Southern accent. I imagine I could live in New York City for fifty years and still talk like this."

"Perhaps."

The doorbell rang, echoing down the hallway. It was only then I noticed the pain along the side of my hand and wrist. Although I had bloody paper towels wrapped around that hand, I'd conveniently forgotten why I wasn't already on the way to the vet.

Anxiety suddenly spun in my chest. "Did you call the police and I didn't even realize it?"

Ryan had started to turn toward the hallway and paused, glancing over his shoulder. "No, Addie. It's not the police. It's a doctor. We'll get your hand looked at and then take Barnable to the vet." Without another word, he turned and strode quickly down the hallway, his footsteps echoing as he moved.

Moments later, a man wearing a beige colored overcoat came striding briskly into the kitchen. "This better be good, Ryan," he said over his shoulder to him. "I was in the middle of dinner."

Ryan simply gestured toward me. "This is Addie Castille. She cut her hand."

The doctor seemed a little warmer than Ryan, his gaze latching onto my paper towel wrapped hand. Plenty of blood had seeped through, and I could imagine I looked ridiculous. My jeans were dirty and wet, I had dirt smeared on both of my arms, and here I was with my filthy dog. Barnable, of course, was happy to greet the newest human in his world. He rose from where he'd been lying on the floor and sniffed around the doctor's feet, wagging when the doctor stroked his back.

The doctor had silvery hair and warm brown eyes. He set a bag on the table. "I'm Dr. Casey. Please call me Daniel. Let's take a look," he said, gesturing for me to step to his side by the counter.

I did as instructed, holding out my hand. Daniel carefully unwrapped the paper towels, turning my hand to the side before peering at me. "This looks like cuts from glass."

I decided to go ahead and fess up. "It is. Ryan thinks I was breaking and entering."

Daniel's eyes widened just slightly before he looked over at Ryan. "Is that so?"

Ryan shrugged. "Her dog broke into my basement first."

Daniel looked back toward me, his eyes twinkling. "Would that be our friendly burglar over there?" he asked, pointing toward Barnable, who'd laid back down on the floor near my feet.

I nodded. "We just moved here, and he got lost. I'm guessing he was scared. It's cold and rainy, and he's not used to the cold at all."

Daniel still held my hand gently in his as he turned away and opened up the bag he'd brought with him. "This is going to sting."

It did, in fact, sting, as he dabbed at the two gashes along my wrist and hand with a cotton ball dampened in some kind of disinfectant.

"Do you mind getting me a towel?" he called as he examined the cuts along the side of my hand.

Ryan didn't respond verbally, but I heard the echo of his footsteps as he turned and left the kitchen. "So, what brings you to New York City?" Daniel asked as he squirted a different liquid on another cotton ball. "This one won't sting as much."

I was relieved to have something to talk about. I was just now starting to realize how tightly wound I was. Finding Barnable was an immense relief. "My great aunt left me her brownstone. I took it as a sign to move here."

The sound of Ryan's footsteps returned to the kitchen, and I glanced over to see him holding two pristine white towels in his hands. He approached and spread them on the counter when Daniel nodded toward it.

"A sign?" Daniel asked.

Glancing to Ryan, I got an arched brow from him. Good grief. Mr. Chatty, he was not. With a mental struggle, I replied, "Yes. I haven't traveled much. I figured it was a sign that I should spread my wings and try something different."

"Where's your aunt's brownstone?" Daniel asked as he rested my hand with the cuts facing up on the towels.

"A few blocks from here."

"Well then, I'd say your aunt was quite wealthy," Daniel murmured as he looked through his bag.

"Oh, she was. She and her husband ran an old department store for many years. Back in the '50s, it was quite popular," I explained.

"About ten years after her husband passed away, she sold the business. I don't really know why she left me her brownstone, but apparently, I was the only child in my generation who wrote to her."

Looking Ryan's way, I saw that he was definitely paying attention with his eyes on me. His expression was so unreadable it flustered me. I always envied those people who could keep a controlled façade. My mother had told me since I was a little girl that I wore my heart on my sleeve and every emotion waving like a flag in the wind.

"Okay, I'm going to put a numbing agent on and stitch these up. If you're queasy at all, I would recommend not watching," Daniel said as calmly as if he was discussing the weather on a sunny afternoon.

"Whaa-aat?" I squeaked. "Shouldn't I go to the hospital for stitches? Maybe just a butterfly bandage or something will do?"

Chapter Three

RYAN

Addie stared at Daniel, her dark eyes opened wide.

Daniel shrugged. "It's certainly not an emergency. If you're concerned, I can assure you I am a fully licensed physician. I'm on call for Ryan's business."

Those dark eyes whipped to me, searching my face. "What in the world do you do where you need a doctor on call?"

"Nothing nefarious, I assure you."

Daniel interjected helpfully, "Ryan runs Talton Tech Industries. It's mostly a tech company, but they do security as well. It's more affordable to have a doctor on call for minor issues that arise. I'm also a friend.

When Ryan called, I came. If you'd like to go to the ER, that's perfectly fine with me."

Addie's gaze bounced to mine again. After a moment, she shrugged. "Fine. I suppose I don't need a hospital bill on top of the police report."

Daniel chuckled, his eyes flicking to me. "Did you call the police on her?"

"No, actually, I didn't. Lord knows why."

"I told you exactly what I was doing as soon as you found me! I can't believe you think if I were actually trying to break in, I would tell you what I was doing. And, Barnable *was* in your basement," Addie protested as she threw her free hand up in the air in frustration.

"All good points. I'm going to start stitching now," Daniel replied calmly.

Addie's eyes dropped to her hand, and her face went white. I didn't even realize what I was doing when I stepped to her side and slid my hand down her back. I was acting on an instinctive need to comfort her. There was a subtle tremor running through her, and she took a shaky breath. "Maybe don't watch," I suggested.

Daniel didn't look up from what he was doing, but I sensed he was quite curious about whatever the hell was going on with me. I sure as hell didn't know. I should've called the police, but it didn't seem Addie meant any harm. As she'd pointed out, Barnable *was* in my basement.

It remained even more puzzling why I'd called Daniel. I hadn't thought about it. It just seemed the quickest thing to do. That said, the most efficient way to extricate myself from the situation would've been to escort Addie and Barnable out. Yet, the idea of sending Addie with her injured hand and her friendly little dog out into the darkness didn't feel right.

Addie looked up at me. "Talk to me about something," she demanded in that Southern drawl that was so damn sexy I didn't even know what to think. My entire body tightened in response to nothing more than the sound of her voice.

Her lashes were so long, they almost brushed against her cheeks as she looked at me. "What should I talk about?" I heard myself asking.

"Something, anything to distract me. Otherwise, I'm gonna keep trying to look, and it feels weird even though it doesn't really hurt."

Rather than talk about myself—because I didn't get personal about myself with many people—I asked, "So, your brownstone is just a few blocks away?"

She nodded, one of her dark curls falling across her forehead. She brushed it away with the back of her wrist.

"Daniel's quite right. Based on location alone, you inherited a gem of a brownstone, no matter the condition. You could sell it and make a pretty penny."

"I don't want to sell it. It's lovely. It does feel a bit like stepping into a time warp, but it seems well maintained. It's just not updated. She left me everything."

"You're from New Orleans?"

Addie wrinkled her nose. "That's what I said earlier. Born and raised there. My entire mother's side of the family is French Creole. As such, I'm fluent in French and grew up steeped in that world. I do love it, and I already miss my family. But I wanted to have a different experience, and New York City is certainly different."

"I haven't been to New Orleans, so I can't say. I'd imagine New York City is quite different. How long have you had Barnable?" I asked as he approached, his short tail vibrating madly as he sniffed my shoes.

"He's almost six years old, and he's my best friend," Addie said solemnly.

"He's pretty good at breaking and entering."

Her lips quirked in a smile at that, and I thought I could handle quite a few more of Addie's smiles. "I suppose it's a hidden talent."

"Okay," Daniel said, finally looking up from Addie's hand. "All done."

He reached for a disinfectant and dabbed over the two areas he'd stitched. Addie's once bloody hand now had two tidy lines of stitches—one running along the edge of her palm and the other up the side of her wrist.

Addie inspected it. "Do I need to make an appointment for when I need to get the stitches out?"

Daniel shook his head. "Nope. They should dissolve. Ryan knows how to reach me, but let me give you my number. If you have any problems, feel free to call my office and stop by."

After Daniel handed Addie his card, I had to force myself to step away from her side. Jesus. She was a physical magnet for me. I'd completely lost my mind.

Daniel looked my way as I walked him down the hallway. "I'm sure I don't need to point this out, but this is entirely out of character for you," he said as I held the door open.

"Fuck off," I muttered.

Chapter Four

ADDIE

"What shall we do today?"

I looked down at Barnable, who was presently napping by my feet at the round table in my aunt Eleanor's kitchen.

Barnable looked up at me and sniffed the air. He'd tolerated a bath from me last night after our adventure to the vet with Ryan. I turned my wrist, eyeing the tidy little rows of stitches. Daniel had done a neat job for such messy gashes. It was a bit sore, but the ibuprofen I'd taken earlier was already easing the pain.

"Barnable, no more running off and breaking into people's basements."

My dog didn't even lift his head from

cleaning his paws for that comment. The vet
had cleaned the scratch on his side last night
and declared it minor. She had looked as curiously at Ryan as I had. He seemed a tad out
of place in his three-piece suit at the vet
clinic. Strangely enough, the vet seemed to
know who he was, although he didn't talk
much while we were there. By that point in
the night, I was just going wherever I was
pointed. It was only this morning that I wondered why Ryan had even accompanied me to
the vet.

Tapping my computer keyboard as I set
my coffee down, I typed Talton Tech Industries into the search bar. A slew of results
came up along with plenty of images. A quick
scan showed me that Ryan was quite the
catch. Most of the photos of him were with
different gorgeous women at a variety of high
society functions. He had mastered the art of
the inscrutable gaze.

I wanted to dive beneath his reserved, arrogant exterior. He'd piqued my curiosity
when he stepped closer to me after I nearly
passed out at the sight of Daniel stitching up
my hand. I liked to think of myself as a
strong woman, but I could admit I'd appreciated Ryan's steady presence when his hand

slid down my back in a warm pass. It hadn't slipped my notice that when I begged him to distract me, he'd simply asked me questions about myself.

I scrolled past the sexy images and tapped on the link to an article titled "Family Feud Ends with Blake Sr.'s Death."

Ryan Blake assumes the helm at Talton Tech Industries upon the passing of his father. Although no one in the family has spoken about the rift between father and son, rumor had it they hadn't spoken for over five years.

Rumors also circulated that Mr. Blake didn't even want to leave the company to Ryan. However, Ryan's maternal grandfather, who founded the company, left an ironclad will in place, leaving Blake Sr. no choice. With the company faltering in the last few years, it will be interesting to see what his son can do to turn it around.

I leaned back in my chair, drumming my fingertips on the table. I lifted my coffee mug for another sip of the rich, dark brew. Ryan appeared to have a bit of a backstory, but then I supposed everyone did. Although I hardly knew him, he had been kind to me last night when he didn't have to be. Maybe he wasn't exactly warm and fuzzy, but he'd gone out of his way to ensure Barnable and I were taken care of. It made my heart ache a little to read about the rumors about his relationship, or lack thereof, with his father.

I didn't mind admitting I was curious. After another sip of coffee, I leaned forward and clicked back into my search window, scanning for a more updated story.

Talton Tech Industries on the rise in investment, technology, and security fields.

"That looks like a good one," I murmured to myself.

Tapping on the link, I scanned it quickly.

Ryan Blake has rapidly restored the fortunes of Talton Tech Industries. While he refuses to comment publicly, he has trimmed down the bloated workforce left behind by his father and shed some investments that were too costly to maintain. Although there were grumblings amongst employees during the first two years, now that the company has turned its fortunes around, it's a prime place to work. The company offers some of the best health insurance anywhere. Although Mr. Blake doesn't speak of it, it's presumed the generous benefits are linked to his brother's health condition, which was costly for their family. His pet projects are mostly in the tech and securities arenas. He continues to donate heavily to various charitable causes.

I clicked back into my search screen and kept scrolling, my gaze latching onto the words "animal shelter" almost instantly. Animal shelter?

I scanned the next article. There were rumors he was a major benefactor to one of the animal shelters in the city. According to this gossip columnist, Ryan refused to acknowledge it, and the shelter refused to disclose their anonymous donor's name.

Although Ryan was nowhere nearby, I started to feel as if I were being a bit too nosy. I closed out of the screen and did a quick check of my email before leaning back in my chair. Glancing to Barnable, whose face was resting between his chubby paws, I commented, "Well, maybe Ryan's a secret dog lover."

Barnable replied with a snore. Considering that my first three days in New York City had been comprised of me running around like a maniac trying to find my dog, I felt at loose ends this morning. I finally had Barnable back, and now I needed to figure out what to do.

My phone buzzed by the kitchen table. Glancing at the screen, I saw my mother's name. I promptly lifted the phone and swiped my thumb across the screen to answer it.

"Hey, Mama. I've got you on speaker, and Barnable is here."

My mother's laugh drifted through the line. "I'm glad to know he's gonna hear my voice. How are you, hon? Feeling better now that you found your boy?"

"Of course."

"Thank you for texting last night to let us know. You know we've been worried about you and him. I told your Aunt Jessie you would probably come home if you didn't find Barnable."

"Definitely not. I would've stayed here until I found him. I'm just glad he didn't get run over by a car."

"As we all are. Now that you can stop worrying, tell me how is Eleanor's place? I haven't been there since we visited when you were a little girl."

I let my mother's soft, Southern accent slide over me, warm and soothing. Although I was excited to be here in New York, the way people talked here was something else. Every word came out fast and staccato. The words themselves were like sharp corners you had to be careful not to run into. It was definitely different from the way people talked in New Orleans.

"Well, I daresay the house might look just

like it did when we visited years ago. It's in excellent condition if a bit dusty. She hasn't upgraded anything. It's like stepping into a time warp. I'd honestly guess she didn't update much after the sixties. She's got one of those refrigerators with those big handles that click when you pull them open," I explained.

My mother laughed. "Well, now that's something."

"Do you think it's okay if I make changes?"

"Of course, dear. You own the house and everything in it," she said firmly.

"I know, but it feels weird. I really didn't know Aunt Eleanor very well, and I never even came here after that time we visited when I was little."

"I don't think that much matters, dear. When you were a little girl, you started sending letters to all of your aunts and uncles. It just so happens Eleanor lived the longest. Although you hadn't seen her since she last came down here when you were a teenager, you were the most like her of all of the grandchildren."

"Really?"

"Oh yes! You've always been a bit of a free spirit, and she certainly was. You're also a bit too independent for my sanity. As you can see, she was too. After her husband, Marcus passed on, she ran that company for a bit before she sold it. Maybe it seems small now, but back then, it was a big deal. Not many women did that and certainly not on their own. Now, you do her proud. For God's sake, get a new refrigerator. I can't even imagine how much electricity that old thing uses," my mother said, tsk-tsking on the phone. "How is Barnable, by the way?"

"Oh, he seems fine. He has a scratch on his side, but the vet said he's fine. I gave him a bath last night."

"And how is your hand?"

I bit back a sigh. I'd mentioned I cut my hand in my text to her last night and had already sent several texts assuring her I was fine. "Mama, it's fine."

"You need to make sure to thank that man. I'm so relieved he didn't call the police on you and Barnable. That could've been a bit of a mess."

"I promise I thanked him. I don't actually know how to reach him, but I do know where he lives. Things are a little different here, though. I'm not so sure it would be okay to stop by."

"Perhaps not."

My mother moved her voice away from the phone. "Yes?" Her voice returned to full volume. "Helen's here," she said, referring to one of her close friends. "I'm gonna go, darling. You call me, okay?"

"Of course. Love you, Mama."

"Love you too, dear."

After hanging up, I stood, scanning the kitchen. The old brownstone had lovely hardwood flooring throughout with tile in the kitchen and the bathroom. I was relieved Aunt Eleanor had skipped the error of updating in the '70s. If she'd gotten trapped in that era, I feared there would be shag carpeting on top of all the hardwood floors. Instead, the brownstone looked like a movie set out of the '60s—furniture, appliances, and so on.

Everything was clean and tidy. A few of the rooms had been repainted. The only benefit to Barnable getting loose was I had thoroughly inspected the house to figure out where he escaped. I'd discovered the lock on the back door was broken. It went out into a lovely little courtyard where he'd likely ventured out through the gate. I'd already arranged for the lock to be repaired, and the gate affixed with a locking mechanism today.

The downstairs was comprised of a large

kitchen on one side, a sitting room, and a formal dining room on the other side of the hallway. There was a small dining area in the kitchen that looked out over the little court-yard in the back. Further down the hallway was a bathroom and laundry room with a door that led into the basement. I presumed the basement of this brownstone was some-thing like Ryan's.

Coffee cup in hand, I padded down the hallway, which led to a pretty entryway. There was a set of double doors with windows flanking it on either side. A staircase hugged the curved wall that led upstairs. I climbed the stairs, taking the time to investigate the three rooms up there. There was a master bedroom with big windows that looked out over the courtyard. It had its own private bathroom and an absolutely lovely clawfoot tub. The other two bedrooms upstairs were smaller with a shared bathroom. I had more space than I knew what to do with.

According to the executor of aunt Eleanor's will, this place currently had a market value of $2 million. He'd given me a look and recommended I consider selling. I had zero intention of selling. I felt like this was where I was supposed to be right now.

After returning to the kitchen, I decided

I'd shower and head out to do some shopping today. It was going to take some work to update everything in this place. I figured I better start with the appliances and go from there.

Chapter Five

ADDIE

A few hours later, I stood in the refrigerator section of a department store dedicated solely to appliances. I was wholly and utterly overwhelmed.

To one side of me, a mother and daughter were arguing. The mother thought the prices were too high, while her teenage daughter thought they should make the refrigerator decision based on looks alone. While I wasn't too worried about money, I did want something reliable.

I spun in a circle, wondering if I could find a salesperson to ask for some guidance. I had eschewed doing so thus far because I'd quickly discovered in the last few days that the moment I spoke, people assumed I had no clue. I was anything but stupid with a graduate degree in fine arts. But my Southern accent gave me away as not being local.

As I scanned the area, my eyes landed on a pair of shoulders encased in a navy suit jacket. I knew those shoulders, the way they stretched the fabric tight across the back, and the way the man's dark hair curled at the collar.

My belly did a little flip.

Good grief, Addie. It's just a man's shoulders. You don't really know that's Ryan.

If my belly could've spoken, it would. Because my belly *knew* that man was Ryan Blake. As if to prove a point, my belly executed a spinning flip when he turned and began walking in my direction.

Ryan walked with purpose, his stride long and brisk. He stopped and glanced up at the signs above the aisles. Another turn and his eyes locked on me.

For a split second—it was so fast I almost missed it—his eyes widened, and I thought he was about to smile. He quickly got control of that impulse, schooling his expression to neutral.

Closing the distance between us in three long strides, he stopped in front of me and inclined his head. "Hello, Addie."

I'd never thought much about a man's voice. Ever. Until I heard Ryan's voice. Dear God. Although he had a typical New York accent, sharp and clipped, the way the words came out with a hint of a rasp sent a shiver chasing through me. Butterflies rose in a mass in my belly and spun in a circle, sending heat scattering like sparks through my body.

All he'd done was say hello. Sweet Jesus.

"Hello, Ryan," I said.

He studied me for a moment, not even bothering to hide the fact that he gave me a full up and down with his eyes. I was wearing a skirt over a pair of wool leggings paired with my favorite cowboy boots. Atop that, I had on a silky blue blouse with my fluffy down coat.

"We're both wearing blue," I announced, rather inanely.

Ryan's eyes landed on mine again, his lips just barely hinting at a smile. I swear to God, he wanted to smile.

As had been the case in my entire life, my mouth got ahead of my brain. "You know you want to smile. Just go ahead. It won't kill you."

His intense gaze studied me for another beat before his smile started at one corner and stretched to the other as he chuckled softly.

Oh God. His voice was one thing, but that low laugh? Downright dangerous. Heat slid like liquid fire through my veins.

As evidence of how thoroughly Ryan had gotten to me, I completely forgot where we were until he spoke again. "How's your hand feeling?"

I lifted my hand and slid my jacket sleeve up just past my wrist. "It's sore, but it looks good."

He leaned over, his eyes scanning over the rows of stitches. Lifting his gaze to mine again, he nodded. "It does look good. I'm sure the soreness will wear off. How's Barnable?"

"He's great. The door is fixed, and he's all settled. Thank you again for your help last night."

"No problem. What brings you to the appliance store?"

"I need a refrigerator," I blurted out as I glanced around me. "There are too many refrigerators to choose from, and I have no idea what to do."

"Did yours break?"

"No, but it doesn't work very well, and I'm pretty sure it's over fifty years old. My great aunt took good care of her place, but I don't think she's updated anything since before I was born."

"You certainly don't look fifty," he countered, a teasing glint in his eyes.

I snorted. "I'm definitely not fifty, just three past half of that, in fact."

Ryan nodded and paused to glance around. "What are you going to get?"

"I have no idea. I've never bought a refrigerator. I don't want to ask a salesperson because I've discovered that everyone assumes I'm stupid."

Ryan's gaze swung back to mine. "Oh, I doubt that. You seem quite sharp to me."

I shrugged. "I'm plenty smart, but my accent gives it up that I'm not from around here. Do you know anything about refrigerators?"

Chapter Six

RYAN

Addie's question echoed in my mind. *Do you know anything about refrigerators?*

I stared at her for probably too long. It didn't help matters that she was so damn sexy. There she stood in her cowboy boots and leggings with a denim skirt. Her fluffy white down jacket was hanging open and revealed a silky blouse where the top button landed a little too low for my sanity.

I could see the tease of her amber skin and a hint of black lace peeking out along the edge of her blouse. Her hair looked windblown. Given that it was, in fact, windy outside today, that might've been my only rational observation. My eyes kept getting caught on her plump lips, her lopsided smile, and that little glint in her dark eyes.

I wasn't used to people teasing me except for a few close friends. Addie was like a bracing breath of fresh air, absolutely nothing like any woman I'd ever encountered. Teasing me about smiling and flinging her hands up in the air over refrigerators.

"I might know a thing or two about refrigerators. What do you want?" I heard myself asking, immediately wondering what the hell I was doing offering up help on refrigerator shopping.

I barely had time to breathe during my days. I'd inexplicably found myself here when the microwave in my office had broken. With my executive assistant out at a personal appointment, I decided to come deal with it myself. There were any number of other people I could've demanded to find me a microwave, but I hadn't been in the mood to explain. So, here I was. Now, apparently, I would also be helping Addie find a refrigerator.

"I just want a regular size refrigerator. I'm all about whatever's the most reliable. I also don't want to spend a fortune if possible," she explained.

She lifted a sheet of paper in her hand and thrust it toward me. "Here's a comparison chart. What do you think? Although, I don't really trust these things either. I don't know how accurate they are."

I scanned the comparison chart and shrugged. "It's fair enough. How about this?" I pointed to one on the list. "It's reliable and basically mid-range as far as cost. It's actually the brand I happen to have in my kitchen if you noticed last night."

Addie peered up into my face and shook her head, a smile teasing at the corners of her mouth. "No. I didn't notice. My hand was bleeding, and I finally found my dog."

"Maybe that or the breaking and entering affected your focus?" I quipped.

Addie's smile broke wide open on her face, and it felt as if a ray of sun splashed over us. "Maybe." She gave a small shrug.

We stood there, for definitely too long, just staring at each other. I didn't know what the hell was going on with me and my crazy reaction to Addie, but I knew I didn't want to let her slip out of my life.

"Excuse me, can I help you?" a voice said.

Addie glanced sideways, blessing the young man who stopped beside us with her smile. My reaction to her was so irrational that I experienced a twinge of envy. I wanted Addie's smile all to myself. I didn't know what that said about me, but I wasn't in the mood to question it.

"Not just yet, but thank you for checking," Addie said before looking back at me. "Show me which one you're talking about."

The man looked curiously between us, but he stepped away when I cast him a look. I was an expert at the kind of look that made people think twice about whatever they might want to say and back off.

Without thinking, I turned and rested my hand on the curve of Addie's lower back, coaxing her forward as I scanned the area until my eyes landed on the refrigerator in question.

"This one," I said, stopping right in front of it.

Addie promptly opened the doors and inspected the inside of the refrigerator. After a moment, she looked up at me with a firm nod. "Okay, I'll get this one."

"You're convinced already?"

"Yes. I trust your opinion on this. Why would you lie to me about a refrigerator? Plus, I know where you live. I can come check."

"On my refrigerator?"

She shrugged lightly. "If I doubted that this was the one you had, yes. I may not know you well, S—" She abruptly cut herself off. "Ryan," she continued, "but I have no doubt you're not going to waste money on an unreliable refrigerator."

"True."

"Hey, what are you doing here? Appliance stores don't really seem the kind of place you'd visit," she commented.

"I'm here for a microwave."

"I bet you already know which one you want."

When she smiled, I felt my own lips curling up. I thought it might be physically impossible not to smile when Addie did.

"I do. I was just trying to find the microwave section."

"I know right where that is," Addie said as she slipped her hand through my elbow and began to tug me along with her.

"How would you know? I can't imagine you've ever been here before today."

"Nope, I haven't. But I came through the back door, and the microwaves are right over there."

Seeing as I didn't mind one bit having the warmth of Addie's hand curled around my forearm as she hurried through the store, I didn't resist being pulled in her wake.

———

My afternoon ended up spent entirely with Addie. After I found my microwave and bought it, I waited while Addie purchased her refrigerator and arranged for delivery that very afternoon.

Because I didn't quite seem to be rational whatsoever when it came to being near Addie, I found myself offering to meet her at the brownstone for the delivery. Although I didn't doubt she could manage it, I did worry about unscrupulous deliverymen. She lived in an upscale neighborhood by herself in a brownstone that, by her own description, hadn't been updated for decades. She was a mark if I'd ever seen one.

There was also her injured hand. Obviously, she needed help. Okay, maybe that wasn't too obvious. Although I couldn't claim to know Addie well at all, my two encounters with her thus far had shown her to be remarkably independent. I had no good excuse for offering to help, at least none I could admit out loud. In all honesty, I simply wanted more time in her presence.

My tendency was toward keeping my life tightly controlled. Work defined my life, and I had few friends. I had learned thoroughly in my childhood that if someone mattered, life could really knock you off balance and yank your heart out of your chest while you were stumbling around. Suffice it to say, I wasn't inclined to let anyone get to me.

Yet, Addie drew me to her in a way no one ever had. She was whimsical, she was funny, and she was sassy. Her spark shined so brightly it lit up my entire life.

I wanted more. That urge brought me into Addie's kitchen late that afternoon. She had shed her fluffy down coat and was torturing me even further because her silky blouse would slip and slide, giving me more than a glimpse of that black lace. I badly wanted to flick her buttons open and trail kisses down the valley between her breasts.

Barnable gave a soft woof when I entered the kitchen. After he sniffed my feet and I greeted him with a few pets, he settled down on a bed in the corner.

I studied the refrigerator she was replacing. "You weren't kidding."

Addie was walking across the kitchen to make coffee. She glanced over her shoulder, her curls bouncing with the motion. "About what?"

"You said you didn't think your great aunt had updated this place in fifty years. I think you might be right. I feel like I've stepped through a door into another era."

Addie tapped the button on the coffee maker and turned back to face me, resting her hips against the counter and curling her hands over the edge. "I know, right? When I inherited this place, I barely remembered what it looked like. We came up here for a visit when I was a little girl, but I was only six years old. My mother doesn't think it's been updated. I sent her a few photos on my phone."

The doorbell echoed down the hallway. "Oh, they're here." Addie walked out of the kitchen.

Barnable stood up and trotted after her. Mindful he'd slipped out and gotten lost before, I followed them to the front hall. "Should we put him in a room?" I called just as Addie reached the front entryway.

"That's a good idea. How about the office right there?" She gestured over her shoulder.

"Come on, Barnable," I said, snapping my fingers. Amicably, he followed along. The office was like the kitchen—everything was untouched and in pristine condition. The desk looked straight out of the 1950s.

"All right, buddy, you stay here," I said as I closed the door behind me once we were in there. Tossing one of the treats Addie had given me earlier to give to him, I left the room.

Addie had already walked the two delivery guys to the kitchen and was presently listening as they marveled at her ancient refrigerator. For the next half an hour while they removed the old refrigerator and brought in the new one, I didn't miss both of the guys taking a gander at her sweet ass, which filled out her denim skirt quite nicely. Like me, anytime she smiled, they appeared temporarily hypnotized.

Meanwhile, I felt like a territorial dog. At one point, I was on the verge of growling. Yeah, this was *so* not me.

Meanwhile, my cell phone was basically blowing up in my pocket. It wasn't like me to leave the office. In my defense, I had not originally left because of Addie. But still.

"I can't thank y'all enough," Addie was saying as we stood in the foyer.

She didn't seem to be aware they might be expecting a tip, so I pulled my wallet out of my pocket and handed one over. "Yes, thank you very much."

They left, blessedly, and Addie glanced over at me. "You didn't have to tip them, but I don't have any cash on me, so thank you. I'll pay you back," she insisted.

"It's not a problem."

"You never did get a chance to have that coffee I offered you when we got here, so come on. I really do appreciate you helping me this afternoon."

As if she had an invisible string attached to me, I simply turned and followed Addie back down the hallway to the kitchen. After she poured me a cup of coffee and I took a few sips, I saw her wince slightly when she moved to set her mug on the counter.

"How's the hand? The whole reason I came to help was to keep you from overdoing it with that," I murmured as I set my coffee down beside hers and stepped closer.

She let me inspect her hand. "It's fine, just a bit sore. I'll take some ibuprofen."

It was only when she looked up at me that I realized just how close we were standing. Maybe only a foot separated us. I wanted to kiss her, so damn badly. My entire body was humming with awareness.

Her dark chocolate eyes searched mine.

The little hitch of her breath in her throat was like a whip cracking through the air. It felt as if time was suspended. I forgot to be wary, the way I typically was. There were so many people prying into my life by virtue of who I was. I rarely, if ever, let my guard down. The strange thing about Addie was she kicked down my walls without much effort.

Lowering my head slowly, I gave her the chance to step away, to bring this crazy spell of lust, fierce desire, and plain insanity on my part to an end.

She didn't. She traced her fingertips along the edge of my jaw. Her light touch was like a tire burning on pavement, scorching over my skin. The mark felt indelible.

"I'm going to kiss you now," I murmured, my voice gravelly.

Addie—because she was bold and sassy—smiled slightly. "Please do."

I brushed my lips across hers, and sparks flashed. Another brush, and then our mouths melted together the moment she arched into me with a soft sigh. Our tongues tangled. What started as a sensual tease exploded as I stepped closer and slid my hand down her spine, finally palming her ass just as I had wanted to do ever since last night. She might've been on her hands and knees trying to break into my basement, but the view of her ass was stamped on my brain.

Addie kissed like a dream. She threw her arms around my shoulders and murmured something before her tongue swiped against mine again. I felt as if I was tumbling into a fire, and I didn't even care if I got burned. Not with Addie warm and soft against me, kissing me as if it were the very thing she'd been meant to do for her entire life.

A muted bark punctured the lust hazing my mind. Another one came, and I recalled Barnable was waiting in the office. It took every ounce of my discipline and sanity to gentle our kiss and draw away. Addie's eyes fluttered open. "Why'd you stop?"

"I believe Barnable is trying to get our attention."

"Oh!" she squeaked, frantically bouncing out of my arms. I let go with reluctance, and closed my eyes as I leaned my hands on the counter while she hurried down the hall, the heels of her cowboy boots echoing with each step.

My cock was so hard it ached. I needed to get a grip. A moment later, after several deep breaths, I thought I had myself under control. I turned when I heard Addie returning to the kitchen and the sound of Barnable's claws on the hardwood floor.

At the sight of Addie with her lips puffy from our kiss and her hair tousled around her shoulders, every cell in my body vibrated to the tune of her. I knelt down to greet Barnable because I needed the distraction.

"Hey buddy, how was the office?" I asked as I ran a hand over his back. He made a snorting sound and circled my legs excitedly.

I looked up when Addie reached for her coffee to take a sip. Straightening, I lifted my cup and drained it quickly. Setting it down, I met Addie's curious gaze.

"I'd like to take you to dinner," I said, surprising myself. I wasn't surprised that I wanted to take her to dinner. Rather, I was surprised I said it aloud.

Addie regarded me across the rim of her coffee cup. "Really?"

"I wouldn't have asked if I didn't want to take you out to dinner."

She wrinkled her nose and set her coffee cup down. "That was a hell of a kiss, but I'm not so sure. S—"

"That's not the first time you started to call me something that starts with "s." Did you forget my name that quickly?"

Addie bit her bottom lip, sending a fresh

jolt of need through me. Her cheeks flushed a little. "When I first met you last night—"

"When I caught you breaking into my basement?" I couldn't help but tease.

Addie threw up her middle fingers and then took another sip of her coffee. "Yes, when you caught me breaking into your basement for an excellent reason. Anyway, I named you Sexy Suit in my head."

I burst out laughing. When I stopped, I shook my head slowly. "I can't say anyone's ever called me that."

"Oh, I'm sure some people have in their head. Don't play dumb, you know you're sexy and handsome. It's obvious you're wealthy. I'm sure you have your pick of women. Now that I know you, I know you might be more than just a suit. You did help me with my refrigerator. You were very gracious about not calling the police on me last night, and you even personally arranged for your doctor friend to take care of me."

"With that list, what's the hesitation on going out to dinner with me?"

I couldn't even believe I'd asked her that. I wasn't used to chasing anyone. I felt knocked off balance.

Addie's dark eyes held mine for a beat.

"You're quite right. I'll be happy to go to dinner with you."

As if he agreed, Barnable trotted over and nudged me in the knees. Leaning down, I scratched behind his ears before straightening again.

"Where and when?" Addie asked.

"If you can believe it, I'll need to check my work schedule. How about you give me your number, and I'll call?"

"I can definitely believe you have to check your work schedule," Addie said with a roll of her eyes.

"Now why would you say that?"

"Because you wear suits like most people wear pajamas. You look totally comfortable, so I'm guessing you spend a lot of time in them."

She handed over her phone after lifting it off the counter and tapping the screen open. "Just put your number in there and text yourself."

I marveled at how trusting she was and did exactly that. A little zing of electricity zipped up my arm when our fingers brushed as I returned her phone.

My phone vibrated for probably the thousandth time today. "Clearly, you need to answer whoever's been texting you all afternoon. I do appreciate your help, but I've noticed your phone buzzes a lot."

Addie took a few steps and leaned up to press a kiss on my cheek. It was a subtle, brief touch, yet it felt as if that one little spot sent sparks scattering through my entire body.

Chapter Seven

RYAN

"Oh no, Ryan wasn't talking late night numbers. He called me over to stitch up the woman who broke into his house," Daniel said with a chuckle before lifting his tumbler of scotch and taking a long swallow.

I glanced to my side, casting him the glare. "You make it sound ridiculous. I was just trying to be helpful."

Graham Morgan glanced between us. "I'm sorry, I don't even understand the situation. I've never known you to call anyone late at night unless it's got something to do with business."

Graham was an old friend. We knew each other from high school. Although we hadn't seen each other much for a few years, we'd gotten close again after my brother passed away. We understood each other well, if only because we both had reasons not to trust others. His ex and former best friend fucked him over, while I had my own baggage from childhood.

He founded Morgan Financial Holdings and had been just as much of a workaholic as me until he fell flat on his face in love and got married. Occasionally, we met for lunch, and I had him manage my investment portfolio. This evening, we met by chance as I was finishing up a business meeting. Graham happened to be here with his beloved wife, Soraya. She waved him off after dinner and told him to stop and have a drink when Daniel paused to chat as well.

"What exactly happened?" Graham pressed, a sly gleam in his eyes.

I took a swallow of scotch. "Well, it is kind of odd. A woman's dog got into my basement through my neighbor's broken basement door. You know how those old basements are. They're all connected under the buildings. Addie heard her dog barking, and I found her trying to get through the window under my stairs."

Graham cocked his head to the side. "Right in front on the sidewalk?" At my nod, he continued. "You didn't call the police?"

I looked toward Daniel. "You met her. Do you think Addie was out to break in my house, or to get her dog?"

"Definitely to get her dog. There's not a criminal bone in her body," Daniel said firmly.

Graham threw his head back with a laugh. "That's a more interesting meeting than I've heard lately. Almost as good as Soraya stealing my phone."

"Wait, Soraya stole your phone?" I asked.

Graham shrugged. "Sort of. I left it on the subway, and she picked it up. That's how we eventually met. I suppose I forgot to tell you that part about how we met. Perhaps your meeting with this woman will prove to be just as fortuitous."

My mind flashed to the feel of Addie's lips under mine during our unexpected kiss the other night.

I shrugged. Although I was irrational enough about Addie that I almost wanted to believe Graham, my well-formed cynicism won for the moment. "Dude, you think everyone's about to fall in love."

Unabashed, Graham shrugged just as there was a vibrating sound.

Daniel patted his suit pocket and slipped his phone out. "Oh, Lynn forgot her keys," he explained, referring to his wife. "I need to go so she can get in the house." He stood from the table. "Always good to see you two. You know where to find me if you want to grab some lunch soon." He began to turn away but looked back at me. "I think you like Addie." With a wink, he strode away quickly.

Graham drained the last of his scotch, his eyes sliding sideways to mine. "Daniel's right. You like her."

"So what if I do?" I countered.

Graham regarded me for a long moment, his gaze assessing. "I hope you do. Considering that you've always said love wasn't worth it."

"Oh, for fuck's sake. Don't get all romantic on me." I wasn't quite sure why I was protesting, but this entire conversation was striking a sore spot.

He shook his head slowly. "You've hardly even made new friends. Not since your brother died."

I rolled my eyes. "You're one to talk."

Graham nodded. "Yup. I get why you'd say that. I'm just saying it's worth letting someone in if it's the right person. Might be good for you." With that, he stood. "Call me soon, okay? Do feel free to let me know the next time a woman tries to break into your house to retrieve her dog," he added with a sly grin.

———

Hazel stared back at me, her steely gaze holding mine without hesitation. "Stop being an asshole," she said flatly.

Aside from a few close friends, Hazel was probably the only person in my world who had the nerve to call me out like this. She had worked for my father for years and had known me since I was a boy. I couldn't imagine running my company without her and was glad she was completely healthy. She was my executive assistant in title, but I paid her far more than the position required because she did so much more.

Reed thin with dark hair flecked with silver and sharp blue eyes, she knew everything about our business and didn't hesitate to keep me on track.

"How am I being an asshole? Do tell."

I leaned my hips against the wall behind me in her office, where I stood beside the door.

"Your uncle was simply calling to check in

and see how you were doing. That's it. You don't need to take out your bottled-up anger at your father on your uncle. He wasn't even on speaking terms with your father for the last ten years of his life."

I rested my head against the wall, taking a deep breath before letting it out. "Fine. I suppose you have a point."

Hazel twisted her mouth to the side and drummed her fingertips on the desk. "Your father *was* an asshole. You're not, so I hate to see you acting like one."

"I'll call my uncle back later this afternoon. First, I need a cup of coffee."

"Shall I get that for you?"

"Thank you, but no. I could use the fresh air," I replied as I pushed away from the wall and opened the door. "I'll be back within a half-hour."

I had a favorite coffee stand a few blocks away and did occasionally leave the office to get some fresh air and coffee. Considering that my work schedule was basically my entire life, these breaks were one of the few luxuries I gave myself.

As I was leaving the building and walking through the massive lower entrance, I caught sight of a pair of familiar boots. Lifting my gaze, I saw Addie striding quickly through the mass of people in the entrance area.

My gaze locked on and tracked her. Today, she wore a pair of jeans that hugged her full hips. She had on her fluffy white down coat. Her long loose curls tumbled about her shoulders. She pushed through the doorway into a law office, one of the few businesses on the lower floor here.

My curiosity zoomed to a peak, and I had to physically resist the urge to follow her into that office. I decided to grab my coffee and come back and wait. I wasn't so far gone that I was going to storm in there after her.

A few short minutes later, during which I almost ran to the coffee stand and back, I leaned against the wall across from the law offices. With a view through the all glass wall, I had a clear line of sight into the reception area. With the amount of foot traffic to pass through this building, I could easily blend into my surroundings. Unless someone recognized me, at a glance, I was just another businessman in a suit.

Moments later, I was rewarded for my patience as I saw Addie step into the reception area from a doorway off to the side. Even from a distance, I could tell she was agitated. She stalked toward the reception desk.

I didn't know what the hell was going on, but Addie was clearly upset. That wasn't okay. Not with me. My feet were moving in the direction of the office before I even realized where I was going. Swinging the glass door open, Addie's voice reached me instantly.

"What the hell? Do y'all think I'm some kind of country bumpkin? You cannot bully me into selling."

Chapter Eight

ADDIE

The haughty receptionist stared at me from behind the desk, her narrow square glasses resting on her skinny nose. "Excuse me?"

"You heard me. I would like to sever my relationship with this law firm, effective immediately. Just hand over whatever paperwork I need to fill out to make sure that happens right this second," I said.

The woman's eyes widened slightly. "Ma'am, did you discuss this with Mr. Huntington?"

"Oh, now you're going to tell me we have to talk to you about it. No, I didn't, I just stormed out of his office, in case you didn't notice."

I felt Ryan's presence before I saw him. He stopped beside me, his hand sliding down my back and coming to rest at the dip in my waist. I was already flustered and furious. While his presence took the edge off in one way, it amped up my nerves in another way.

"Is everything okay?" he asked, his tone low.

When I glanced up at him and met his eyes, a little jolt of electricity zapped my system. His gaze was concerned. Of course, my body's instantaneous reaction to him only flustered me further. My belly spun in flutters, and I swallowed as goosebumps broke out over my skin. I felt hot and cold all over.

"No. Actually, it's not. I'm firing this law firm," I announced. I might've been flustered, but I could stay focused when I was angry.

When I looked back at the uptight receptionist, it was obvious she recognized Ryan. "Mr. Blake, there's simply been a misunderstanding. I'm trying to reach Mr. Huntington right now as we speak. Oh, look, there he is," she said brightly.

"Cute," I replied. "I'm sure you'd like me to keep this scene private. I'm not interested. You're fired," I said as I spun to look at the attorney.

Suddenly, everyone who couldn't be bothered with me and had been trying to push me around for the last few meetings I'd had here became obsequious.

"Now, Ms. Castille. Clearly, we misunderstood your needs. Let's discuss this privately," Mr. Huntington said. He wore a suit, just like Ryan. However, he didn't wear it nearly as well. Mr. Huntington looked in Ryan's direction. "Mr. Blake. Good to see you. We've had a minor misunderstanding with—"

Ryan cut him off abruptly. "Doesn't sound like it's a misunderstanding to me. It sounds like she's firing you."

"Thank you!" I exclaimed. "At least someone understands me around here."

Ryan glanced from Mr. Huntington to the receptionist. "If any paperwork needs to be filled out to formally sever Ms. Castille's legal representation, please call my office within the next fifteen minutes. I'll have someone take care of the paperwork immediately."

At that, Ryan moved with me as I turned and stalked out of the office. When the glass door closed automatically after we stepped out, I glanced up at Ryan. "I can't even slam the door! So unsatisfying," I huffed.

He flashed me a roguish grin. "Oh yes. I can see how that would make it all better."

"They're assholes."

"So it seems. Come up to my office with me. I'll have my assistant take care of any paperwork for you and then let's go have dinner."

I glanced at my watch, pushing the sleeve of my down coat out of the way. "It's only five o'clock. Isn't that early for dinner?"

"I don't think so. If you want to quibble over time, you can sit with me for happy hour and dinner," he replied swiftly.

I found it difficult to say "no" with Ryan's blue eyes on mine, and his hand a heated brand at the base of my spine.

I didn't realize I was nodding affirmatively until a slow smile curled the corners of his mouth and sent my pulse into overdrive. Sweet Jesus. Ryan's smiles were delectable and dangerous at once. I managed a shallow breath. With my body already revving from my confrontation with the attorney, my pulse lunged.

"Come upstairs with me," he said, exerting a gentle, coaxing pressure on my back as he turned and guided us toward the bank of elevators. He held a cup of coffee in his free hand.

I meant to tell him he didn't need to help me with this. Not that I had any clue who I would call about it, but surely I could find an attorney. However, once we stepped into the elevator, we were joined by another cluster of people, which eliminated any privacy. This was a massive high-rise building, and I imagined there were plenty of offices on every floor.

I felt some curious glances cast in our direction and guessed Ryan was recognizable to a few people. He stayed quiet, exuding a do-not-disturb air. The elevator zoomed skyward. By the time we made the last stop, there were still several people left with us, and I realized Ryan's offices were on the uppermost floor in the building. When we stepped out of the elevator, the others scattered in different directions, while I simply followed where Ryan guided me. As unsettled as I was by his presence, somehow his touch was an anchor in my internal tumult. He was steady and calm. I needed that.

Talton Tech Industries was emblazoned across the door in steel gray lettering. I started to reach for the door handle, but Ryan's voice stopped me.

"How's your hand?"

Glancing to him, I lifted it. "It's fine. Hardly sore at all." I angled it to the side as my sleeve slid up.

He leaned over to inspect the stitches.

Most of the redness had faded, and the stitches were already absorbing into my skin. Lifting his eyes to mine, he nodded. "Good." Without another word, he opened the door.

Ryan's hand dropped away from me as he gestured me through. I instantly missed his touch. He nodded toward the receptionist.

"Hello, Mr. Blake," she offered with a smile.

"Hello," was his only reply.

Ryan's warm hand landed on my back again, and I bit back a sigh. It shouldn't feel this good to have his subtle touch on me, but it was decadent, and I savored it.

His office was all cool grays and blues with a slightly warm touch from watercolor paintings on the walls. Our footsteps were muted as he led me through the reception area and down a hallway. We stepped through a doorway where there was another receptionist.

This woman looked up, her sharp gaze bouncing from Ryan to me. "I didn't know you had a meeting, Ryan," she said with a curious smile.

"That's because I didn't have a meeting. Hazel, this is Addie Castille," he said with a nod between us. "Addie, this is Hazel. She's my assistant, and she basically runs my life."

"Nice to meet you," I said with a smile.

Hazel cocked her head to the side as she stood and rounded her desk. " It's a pleasure to meet you. Is your name an abbreviation?" she asked as she held her hand out.

Reaching out to shake her hand, I felt as if she was assessing me from head to toe. In fact, Hazel didn't even bother to hide it with her eyes sweeping over my hair, down to my cowboy boots and back up. I sensed she was absorbing every single detail about me.

As she dropped my hand when her eyes met mine again, I replied, "Addie is short for Adelaide."

"Oh, what a lovely name."

"Thank you. It's French."

"I would have guessed that. What brings you here?"

"Well..."

Ryan interjected, "Actually, I brought Addie up here. I was hoping you could give us a little assistance."

"Since my title is your executive assistant, obviously, I am here to assist you however you need," Hazel replied cheekily.

I guessed Hazel knew Ryan quite well, considering that he was entirely unruffled by the hint of sarcasm in her tone. He chuckled, cementing my thinking. "You are, in fact, my assistant. Addie just fired the attorney for her great aunt's estate. They're in the office on the main floor. They might try to make things difficult. I was hoping you could call out to the attorney we have on retainer to help with matters like this and make sure whatever needs to be handled gets handled."

Hazel gave me a curious glance as she nodded. "I'm happy to help. Can you give me a little background, so I know what to explain to the attorney?" she asked, directing her question to me.

"Oh yes. I hope you don't think I expected Ryan to help me. He kind of insisted." I cast him a glance.

"I'm well aware Ryan can be pushy. I hope this is what you want." Hazel swung her eyes over to Ryan. "You didn't fire her attorney, did you?"

Ryan rolled his eyes and looked to the ceiling. "I'm not *that* pushy."

"I fired the attorney. I promise. Ryan came in while I was storming out of the offices downstairs on the first floor," I hastily explained.

Ryan commented from my side. "I'm going to finish up a few things in my office. If you'll bring Addie in once you're done, that would be great."

Hazel looked at him and nodded. "Of course."

Ryan's cell phone chimed, and he slipped it out of his pocket. With a quick nod in my direction, he turned and crossed the room to step through a doorway. My eyes tracked him, lingering on the easy swing of his shoulders and the way his suit fit him so deliciously well.

I'd promised myself I was never going to let myself fall for a man so far out of my league. Ryan was practically on another planet as leagues went. Yet, I was about to go out to dinner with him. On the list of not-very-smart choices, that was high.

When I looked back toward Hazel, I caught her watching me watching Ryan. I felt the flush heat my cheeks and silently swore.

I rushed into explaining. "I know Ryan asked you to help me, but if it's too much trouble, you don't need to do anything. I have no problem letting Ryan know he doesn't need to swoop in and take care of everything for me."

"Addie, I'm happy to help. Just give me a quick sketch of the situation. Then, when I call our attorney, I can adequately explain what's going on. Please have a seat." Hazel gestured to one of the chairs directly across from her desk.

I sat down and took a deep breath to steady myself. Between losing my temper with the attorney and this encounter with Ryan, I needed a few minutes to regain my composure.

Hazel tapped on her keyboard and glanced over. "Okay, what shall I tell the attorney?"

"To make a very long story short, I inherited my great aunt's brownstone in the Upper West Side. Apparently, it's quite valuable. I wouldn't know because I grew up in New Orleans. I also inherited her entire estate. That's all well and good. While I'm sad Aunt Eleanor passed away, she lived a good life. She was almost eighty-five years old."

"I'm sorry for your loss, dear. If I understand from what little Ryan had to offer, the attorney you just fired was the one responsible for your aunt's estate, correct?"

I nodded. "Yes. It's all tidied up, but they keep trying to get me to sell the house, and I don't want to sell. Honestly, I feel like they're trying to take advantage of the situation, but I'm not quite sure how. It doesn't matter what I say, they keep dragging things out and trying to make me sell. I would like someone to look over everything so I can make sure that nothing is amiss, and I don't want them handling the estate anymore."

Hazel cast me a quick smile. "I do like you. I like that you had no trouble standing up to them. I can't say I know much about that firm. I'll call over to the attorney Ryan uses to handle his estate business and see what they have to say. I assume if you want representation, you'll need to sign some paperwork. Do you want me to help take care of that?"

"Don't take this the wrong way, but just because they listen to Ryan doesn't mean they'll listen to me." I wasn't sure what was best right now, so I figured honesty was my only option.

"I definitely understand your point. How about we start with you signing something that'll just give them the authority to look everything over? They can handle the transfer from the other firm, and you can go from there?"

"Sounds good."

In short order, Hazel spoke with the attorney and had me sign something. By the time we were done, I already had a meeting arranged with the new attorney for later this week.

Hazel was returning to her desk after filing something when she paused at the side and rested her hand on the glossy wood surface. "I may be too forward, but I'd like to share something with you."

Considering I was clueless about what she was talking about, I simply nodded.

"There's much more to Ryan than meets the eye. He can come across as—" She paused, drumming her fingertips on the table.

"Uptight?" I helpfully interjected.

Hazel laughed softly and nodded. "Yes. That would be one word I might use. Given his success and position in society, he's accustomed to people wanting things from him. He's quite private and can come across as cold and uninterested. He's not, though."

Uncertain how to take what Hazel had chosen to share with me, I took a moment and then decided to just be myself. "If you're worried I want something from Ryan, you needn't worry. As you can see from just a glance—" Pausing, I swept a hand up and down in front of me. "I'm not exactly running in the same circles as he is. Or so I would imagine."

"Oh dear. If you think I was warning you away from him, you're quite mistaken. I was trying to convey that I hoped you wouldn't jump to conclusions about him. I like you, and I think Ryan likes you. He could use someone such as yourself in his world. Very few people have the nerve to talk back to him."

"You do," I offered.

Hazel's return grin was sly. "That I do. I've known Ryan since he was a boy, and I know what his family life was like. He's lost a lot. He's certainly not the heartless asshole he sometimes tries to convey to the world. Give him a chance. Now, follow me." She turned quickly, giving me no further opportunity to comment.

I followed her down a short hallway. Stopping in front of what I presumed was Ryan's office door, she nodded quickly before opening it.

"Addie is all set," she called.

When Hazel gestured me through the door, I stepped into his office. Ryan was on the phone, but he glanced up and lifted a finger to indicate he might be on the phone for a moment.

"Go ahead and have a seat," Hazel said softly before pointing toward a set of chairs situated in front of floor to ceiling windows that looked out over Manhattan.

Without another word, the door closed with a whisper behind me, and my heart started drumming inside my chest.

Chapter Nine

ADDIE

Ryan's eyes tracked me as I walked across his office. Stopping beside the windows, I heard him saying, "Jack, I'll need to get back to you on this. I have a meeting."

I presumed Jack on the other end of the line was saying something as Ryan fell quiet. Tuning him out, I scanned the view beyond the windows. It was kind of remarkable to me how different New York City felt from New Orleans. While New Orleans was filled with energy and the mingled cultures of the South, French, Creole, the jazz world, and more, New York City exuded the vitality of business, motion, sharp voices, and a combination of cultures that was almost overwhelming.

Looking out over the skyline, it all seemed rather stark with skyscrapers of steel towering over concrete with the Atlantic Ocean stretching out in the distance. Slowly turning, I let my eyes scan his office. Muted blues and grays continued from the outer office. There were no personal touches in here, not a single photograph of a human being anywhere. There was a watercolor mounted on the wall, which was soothing with its lavender flowers blurring into a blue sky.

Ryan and his suits were such a contrast to me. My eyes landed on the toes of my cowboy boots and then a few of Barnable's hairs on my knee from when he rubbed against my calf this morning. Without thinking, I brushed the fur off my jeans before realizing I'd just brushed it onto Ryan's pristine gray carpeting.

Glancing up when Ryan hung up the phone, I blurted out, "Shit! I just got dog fur on your carpet. I'm sorry."

My words seemed to take Ryan off guard. He stared at me for a beat as he stood from his desk and crossed the room to stop in front of me. "No need to worry. It's doubtful anyone will notice. If it makes you feel better, we have cleaning staff come through here every night. I'm sure they'll vacuum up Barnable's fur," he said, a slow grin that did crazy things to my belly unfurling.

I decided right then and there that Ryan shouldn't be allowed to grin, not without a warning first. I'd never had a man affect me the way he did, and I certainly didn't know what to do about it. There was a well-planted kernel of doubt in my heart and in my mind. I'd spent my childhood witnessing my mother long for a man who didn't quite fit in her world. That man was my father, and he never looked back after he left her pregnant. Oh, he paid his bills, but that was it. I'd promised myself I'd never be that foolish.

Ryan certainly wasn't my type. Or better yet, I *knew* I wasn't his type. I had resisted the urge to look him up online since my first foray. Still, I hadn't forgotten the glamorous and classically beautiful women at his side from those photos at high society functions.

Because I was me, and I never shied away from saying what I thought even when I was nervous, I jumped right onto that thought like it was a train that would zoom me out of here. "Look, I appreciate your help with the attorney situation, but we shouldn't go to dinner."

Ryan's gaze swept over me, his blue eyes holding mine. Restless and feeling as if he were trying to see right into me, I shifted on my feet and broke away to look out the window. "You have a lovely view," I added rather inanely.

I felt Ryan step to my side. Unable to stop it, my eyes slid sideways, taking in the chiseled lines of his face. He had a bold profile with a strong square jaw, almost harsh cheekbones, and a straight blade of a nose. His full sensual lips served to soften the edges. Suffice it to say, nature had been kind to Ryan Blake.

He turned, catching me studying him. I didn't care about that so much. I presumed he was accustomed to it.

"Now, why would you say we shouldn't go to dinner?" he asked as he faced me fully.

I gestured to him. "Ryan, you wear suits. Very well, I might add. I tend to wear boots and jeans and sometimes skirts and leggings. I just don't think we fit together."

A dark brow slashed upward as Ryan regarded me. "I wear suits for business. It's not a style choice. Even if it was, is there some kind of thing where all men who wear suits can only date certain types of women? Don't even try to argue the point that our kiss the other night wasn't hot for you."

Perfect. Exactly what I needed to

strengthen my attitude. Resting a hand on my hip, I tilted my head to the side and arched a brow, mimicking him slightly. "Cocky much?"

"That's not me being cocky," he said flatly. "That kiss nearly set me on fire, and you don't strike me as the type of woman to fake any kind of response. If you were, go ahead and tell me now. I know chemistry when I feel it."

My cheeks got hot. I wasn't going to argue about that kiss. My God. I must've replayed that kiss a few hundred times already. Crossing my arms, as if I could somehow contain the wild beating of my heart, I let out a sigh. "Fine. So it was a great kiss. Since when did desire lead to good decisions?"

Ryan shrugged. "I don't know, and I don't really care. I know I want you more than I've ever wanted anyone, and I'd like to take you to dinner."

When he stepped closer, I felt my heart move in my chest, as if there were an actual magnetic force drawing me closer to him. I feared he was going kiss me again, and I'd melt into a puddle at his feet right here in his office—because kisses from Ryan were guaranteed to turn me to butter. My apprehension cued me in to just how desperately I wanted him.

He didn't kiss me, though. Oh no. He simply caught one of my hands in his. The feel of his warm grip curling around mine, then his thumb brushing in slow passes over the back of my palm, made my knees weak and butterflies burst to life in my belly.

Oh my word. I was in deep, deep trouble. I swallowed and managed a ridiculously shallow breath. "Okay. I'll go to dinner," I said, my voice coming out just above a whisper.

Ryan's lips curled at one side and his grin unfurled slowly—that dangerous, delicious grin of his that sent sparks scattering throughout me until I was tingling all over.

"We can stop by my place first. I'll change out of my suit if that'll make you feel better."

I shook my head wildly. "Oh no. Stay in the suit. You really do wear it quite well," I managed to tease.

"Let's go then."

Without releasing my hand, he turned and began walking toward his office door. I planted my cowboy boots firmly in place and tugged on his hand. "Just a second."

Ryan turned around to face me. I was learning that when he gave me his attention, it was complete, and it drove me a little crazy.

"We're not having sex," I blurted out, snapping my mouth shut as soon as the words escaped.

I stared at Addie, watching as her pretty mouth fell open in a little O shape before she snapped it shut.

"Excuse me?" I countered.

Although her cheeks were flushed pretty and pink, Addie lifted her chin. It had a stubborn tilt to it, and I didn't doubt for even half a second that Addie could be stubborn.

"I said we're not having sex," she repeated, each word enunciated clearly in that delicious southern drawl of hers.

"We're having dinner. Just dinner, Addie. Although I can't help but wonder why you feel the need to clarify we aren't having sex."

Her chin lifted higher, and her eyes narrowed. "Just thought I should establish the boundaries."

"Understood."

As we walked into the small area outside my office where Hazel's desk was, I glanced her way. "I'll see you tomorrow morning."

"Thanks again for your help, Hazel," Addie chimed in.

I didn't miss the twinkle in Hazel's eyes as they flicked down to where my hand clasped Addie's. I knew I'd hear about this tomorrow. The fact that I was holding any woman's hand could be considered newsworthy of gossip around the office. Hazel wasn't one to gossip, but she'd been on my case for years about not working so hard and not treating every woman I took out as a transaction. Her words, not mine. There was also the fact that I was actually leaving work at a reasonable hour. Working until nine p.m. was the norm for me. I was usually the last one to leave.

Hazel addressed Addie first as we paused in front of her desk. "It was my pleasure, Addie. It was very nice to meet you. If you need anything, please do call. I can't even imagine what it's like to be new in a city like this."

"Oh, that's sweet. Thanks so much," Addie replied with one of her wide smiles that made my heart squeeze a bit.

Hazel's eyes swung to me, and I could see curiosity spinning in her gaze. "I'll see you in the morning."

With a nod, I led Addie to the door, holding it open as she walked through. Just as I released it, Hazel's voice reached me. "Nice to see you leave at a reasonable hour."

I bit back a chuckle. I should have known Hazel couldn't resist commenting.

———

I watched as Addie lifted her wine glass. My eyes trailed down the length of her neck when she tilted her head back and took a swallow. I hadn't forgotten the taste of her lips underneath mine, and I was desperate to taste her skin.

My mind kept rolling back to Addie's blurted comment about not having sex. I had no problem taking things slow. Yet, I was forced to admit I was more accustomed to being the one who set the ground rules and boundaries. Not that I thought I was all that great of a catch. I didn't, per se. However, I was sensible enough to know that, as a billionaire in Manhattan, there were always people who wanted something from me. I went out of the way to cultivate a reputation of someone who wasn't interested in anything beyond business-like dating relationships.

For the first time—ever—I wanted more. Much, much more. I sensed I was going to have to work for it with Addie.

Setting her wine glass down, Addie leaned back in her chair. I'd taken her to an old favorite restaurant of mine. I was the one who looked out of place in my suit here. It was a bit of a hole in the wall type of diner that served classic fare. They had a rotating selection of dinner specials that were surprising and refreshing. I hadn't let myself contemplate this choice. It was a place I'd frequented with my late brother many times when we were younger.

Much as I wanted Addie, I wasn't ready to contemplate what it meant that I took her to a place that held such sentimental meaning to me. My brother had probably been one of the few people in my life I'd truly loved. Kicking those thoughts to the curb, I focused on Addie.

Her curls fell in a messy tumble around her shoulders, and her dark eyes were contemplative. Unlike places with what you might call ambiance, the lighting here wasn't meant to compliment or obscure. It was on the bright side and almost harsh. Still, Addie glowed. She leaned on her elbows, and my eyes caught on the tiny freckles dotting her cheeks. I'd noticed them the other night. They were just barely there, fairy dust scattered over her cheeks almost as an afterthought and blending into her amber skin.

She'd shrugged out of her down jacket, revealing another silky blouse. That seemed to be a preference of hers. I appreciated it, yet it was a temptation to my sanity. Tonight, she wore a deep plum silk. Every time she shifted, I was teased with hints of her cleavage and black lace.

She wrinkled her nose as she regarded me. "This was not the kind of place I expected you to take me for dinner," she announced.

"No?" I hedged. It felt as if she had somehow dived straight into my earlier train of thought from moments ago.

"Of course not. Don't play dumb. I'll admit I looked you up. It was the morning after I almost broke into your basement, so I was kind of curious. Don't worry, I didn't get crazy and stalk you. But I know you're a billionaire. I know you turned your family's company around. I also know there are tons of photographs of you at important social functions with beautiful women. I would've expected you to take me somewhere fancy and hoity-toity."

"Did I disappoint you?" I countered, unable to resist a grin tugging at the corners of my mouth.

"Oh no. I do love good food. This was delicious and far more down to earth than I expected. I'm just curious. You also seem to know the people who I think are the owners."

I took a swallow of my scotch. Although this diner served classic fare, they also had a full bar in the evenings. That might seem off, but this was New York City and alcohol brought in more customers. I shifted my shoulders in a subtle attempt to ease the tension instantly bundling at the back of my neck. That tension was precisely why I tried to keep things impersonal.

Addie was different though, so I brushed through the shadows crowding my thoughts. I took a deep breath and another swallow of my scotch. "It's an old favorite place. I do know the owners, Johnny and Angie. My brother and I used to come here a lot."

I rarely spoke about my brother except among people who'd known him. Merely saying the word "brother" out loud elicited a painful thump of my heart.

Addie was quiet for a moment, her eyes searching my face. "I feel like there's more to the story than that. Where is your brother now? Does he still live in New York City?"

"He's buried here."

Addie's eyes widened, understanding crossing her face quickly. She reached across the table and curled her hand over mine, her touch light and warm. "Oh my goodness. I'm so sorry."

Her words were so heartfelt and so earnest that the ache around my heart eased a bit. "Thank you. We were close, so, well, it wasn't easy."

At that moment, Angie paused by our table. Her sharp brown eyes swung from me to Addie and back. She had a tray stacked with plates resting on one forearm. I'd known Angie since I was a boy. "How are you two doing?" she asked in her rapid speech. "Need anything?"

Addie's hand slipped off mine as she looked up. "No, but thank you."

"We're all set. You can bring the bill when you have a sec," I added.

"Be back with it shortly," Angie said, spinning away when another customer called her name.

Addie was quiet for a moment. I was relieved by that interruption. I needed something to push me through to the other side of the mention of Colin.

"What happened?" Addie asked, her tone soft.

"Ewing's sarcoma. He was diagnosed when he was fourteen. He died when I was twenty-eight, the year before my mother died, and then my father died. My entire immediate family died within three years of each other."

I didn't often speak of my family, so the words came out rote and flat. Addie's eyes widened, glistening with tears. Meanwhile, I felt as if a cold wind had gusted through my heart and soul. While I missed Colin deeply, my parents, not so much. Their marriage was exactly why I'd told myself for many years I never wanted to pursue romance. Cold and bitter didn't even capture the state of their marriage.

"I'm so sorry," Addie finally said. "That's a lot of loss. How long ago was that?"

I knew precisely how long. "Five years since my brother died. I'm okay, Addie. Colin's death was the hardest. I wasn't close to my parents. I don't know how much you read about me in your online search, but that's not a secret."

She was quiet for a long moment, her fingertip tracing circles in the moisture on her water glass. It was only when she moved to turn the glass and trace on the opposite side that I noticed she'd actually drawn a flower.

I smiled before I even realized it.

"What are you smiling about?" she asked.

Glancing into her concerned eyes, I nodded toward her water glass. "You drew a flower."

She still didn't smile, her gaze sweeping over mine. "I did. Just a habit. Are you okay?"

"I'm not going to pretend this is a pleasant topic, but yes, I'm fine. I'd rather not dwell on it if you don't mind."

She held my gaze for several beats before nodding slowly. "I certainly don't mind. It's just I'm really close to my family, so that would be devastating for me."

"And yet, you moved all the way to New York City all by yourself," I commented, genuinely curious.

Addie smiled. "I did, but I miss them. I talk to my mother every day."

"Every day?"

She nodded unabashedly. "Yep. I came to New York City because I wanted to see the world and do something different. Geographic distance doesn't change how much I love my family."

"Any brothers and sisters?"

"Nope. Just me. I was actually an accident. My mother was told she couldn't get pregnant, and then I came along. I have a massive extended family in New Orleans, hundreds of cousins probably. I should mention that while I'm close to my mother, I barely talk to my father. He was never around when I was growing up."

That detail surprised me. "Oh?"

Addie shrugged. "An absentee father isn't the worst thing. It just is what it is." She paused for a moment before she added, "I'm really sorry about your brother. Maybe you weren't close to your parents, but I'm sorry about that too."

"Thank you."

Angie arrived and handed me the check. "Always good to see you, Ryan. You take care now."

Slipping my wallet out of the inner pocket of my suit jacket, I handed over several bills without even checking to see how much. I made a habit of overpaying here, usually by a hundred or more dollars. "Keep whatever change there is. It's always a pleasure to see you, Angie."

"You should stop by more often," she replied.

"I will."

With a quick smile, Angie hurried on to the next table, filling coffees and moving about the busy diner. As I stood from the table and walked out with Addie, I felt strange, almost as if Colin were here with me for a moment. He would approve of Addie. I had no doubt about that. He would not approve of the various women I kept at a distance. Given that he'd spent more than half of his life facing down a serious and eventually terminal illness, he wasn't much for casual.

Chapter Eleven

RYAN

We stepped out into the cold February night. Addie pulled her jacket tightly around her shoulders. "It's going to take some getting used to these winter nights."

When she peered up at me with the streetlights glittering above in the frosty darkness, my heart gave two rapid thumps inside my chest. Without thinking, I leaned down. "It's not so bad," I murmured, right before I brushed my lips over hers.

I wanted Addie. So fucking much.

It felt as if electricity spun through me in a fiery jolt from where our lips met. I drew back, just slightly.

Addie looked up at me, her dark eyes flashing under the soft glow from the streetlight above us. Considering it was New York City and only maybe nine at night, the street was by no means empty. People walked along the sidewalks and passed around us, yet somehow it felt as if we were all alone in the world, enclosed in this tiny moment.

The temporary spell was broken when someone bumped into Addie as they walked briskly by. Just because I needed her touch, almost as if it were a dose, I leaned down once more and pressed a kiss to Addie's lips. The temptation to let it unfurl into so much more hovered right there, but I pulled back when someone's elbow hit my back.

"Come on," I said as I straightened. "I'll walk you home."

As I turned, I almost curled my hand around her injured hand. I caught myself in time and immediately shifted to her other side before taking her hand.

She glanced up as we began walking. "My hand really isn't that sore anymore."

"Good to hear. It looks much better."

"It's a little itchy, but that means it's heal-ing. All's well that ends well with my burglary attempt," she said, her tone dry.

I chuckled. "All you were trying to steal was your dog. How is Barnable? Is he settling in?"

"Oh yes. He's a good boy. I think he just slipped out of the gate because he was curious, and then he got lost. I've got the back courtyard locked up tight now."

"Good to know."

We walked in silence the rest of the way to Addie's place. When we climbed her steps together, a sense of protectiveness washed through me. I knew that this place her great aunt had left to her was valuable. Living only a few blocks away, I was acutely aware of the property values in this area. It bothered me to consider that the attorney's office was probably pushing her to sell, most likely to try to profit off the sale. As executors of her aunt's estate, they might be trying to take advantage of the situation and assume Addie didn't know much about the area. I didn't like it. Not one bit.

We were greeted by a gruff bark from Barnable on the other side of the door as Addie fit her key in the lock. "He's a good doorbell," I observed.

Addie smiled up at me. The moment we stepped through the door, Addie knelt down to greet Barnable. After several pets from her and a hello from me, he trotted back down the hallway, his claws clicking rapidly on the hardwood floors.

I'd told myself I'd walk Addie home, say good night, and leave. Although I knew I wanted her, I wasn't prepared for the depth of my reluctance to leave her. I did *not* want to go.

I could've tried to tell myself it was about sex. It wasn't though. I simply enjoyed spending time with her. She was warm and funny, and so perfectly herself. I was accustomed to people in business and social events trying to create an impression for me. That was why my circle of true friends was so small.

It often felt as if every social interaction was a calculation. People like Addie were few and far between in my life. Addie made no effort whatsoever to be anything other than herself.

Addie set her purse on the small table beside the door, dropping her keys beside it before she turned to face me. The sound of her cowboy boot heels striking the floor when she took a step closer to me echoed around us. She placed her palm on my chest, and my heart lunged toward her touch.

"One more kiss," she said, the sweet twang to her words sliding over me and spinning into the need already tightening every cell in my body.

"I'd better make it count then," I replied as I placed my hand over hers.

With a gentle nudge from me, Addie stepped back until she stood against the door. Lacing my fingers with hers, I lifted our joined hands, pressing them against the door just above her shoulder. The sound of her breath hitching in her throat sizzled through me like a bolt of lightning.

My response to Addie was something entirely unfamiliar to me. I didn't lack for sexual experience. However, I was accustomed to feeling in control of myself.

With her, all we'd shared was one crazy hot kiss and a few brief, almost chaste kisses tonight. And yet, I felt as if I were scrambling for purchase on the edge of a cliff, about to fall over. I already knew when I did fall, if there was a rope to catch, it would be frayed and about to snap.

Addie's tongue darted out and swiped across her bottom lip. Another jolt sizzled through me. When she took a deep breath, her breasts pressed against my chest, and I practically had to talk myself down. Much as I wanted more, more than that, I didn't want to rush through anything with her.

I also hadn't forgotten Addie's declaration that we couldn't have sex. She was giving me one kiss, and I intended to make it a kiss for the ages.

Lifting my free hand, I cupped her cheek, tracing my thumb over her plump bottom lip. "I like you, Addie." My words came out in a gruff whisper.

She took another little breath, her eyes on mine the entire time. "Against my better judgment, I like you too," she whispered, something flickering in the depths of her eyes, something I didn't quite know how to interpret.

For just a second, I sensed someone had hurt her. Knowing nothing about it, I experienced a cold chill. If anyone did hurt her, I wanted to make them pay the price for it. That price would be high.

It was also something I couldn't deal with just now. Right this second, I had Addie pressed against me, and she'd granted me one kiss. That kiss was absolutely *all* that mattered in this moment.

Dipping my head, I brushed my lips over hers, watching as her eyes fluttered closed on a sigh. Her fingers tightened into mine. On the heels of her next sigh, I angled my head to the side and fit my mouth over hers.

The moment her tongue slid sensually against mine, any idea I had of controlling the pace burned into nothing. Addie tasted sweet, and kissing her was like diving into a fire. I didn't care if the burn devoured me. With slow sweeps of my tongue, my hand slid around her nape. She made this soft sound in the back of her throat, and it drove me insane.

My fingers laced more tightly with hers as we held onto each other. When her hips rocked into me, with my cock rock hard and tight in the confines of my slacks, I groaned deep in our kiss. I couldn't get enough of her.

I meant for this kiss to be a seduction, to be something she would never forget. Instead, I was prey to the sheer force of my need for her. My hand slid out of her hair, brushing over her shoulder before pushing her coat apart. Her silk blouse was warm from the heat of her skin.

I drew my fingers lightly in a circle over the taut bead of her nipple pressing against the silk. Satisfaction washed over me as I teased her. I felt the force of my need spinning faster inside and sensed I might be about to take things too far. It took all of my discipline to slam the brakes on this.

I tore my lips away from hers, resting my forehead against hers as the sound of our ragged breathing filled the space around us.

Chapter Twelve

ADDIE

I felt the cool wood of the door behind me filtering through my coat. It was a contrast to the enveloping heat of Ryan's body pressed against the front of me from head to toe. My thoughts were all a muddle, tumbling about in my mind as I tried to gather myself together.

I told him he could have just one kiss. I had greatly underestimated just how devastating one kiss from Ryan could be. I felt as if I were flying apart with my need vibrating through me and sparks scattering everywhere. I was almost frantic inside.

Part of me was distantly alarmed at my state. Ryan was too much of everything. My rational mind was subdued, practically beaten into submission by the force of my desire. Even then, I still knew Ryan wasn't a smart choice for me. But my body—and apparently my treacherous and way too stupid heart— had other ideas about him. My body thought he was the best thing ever. He was a man who kissed like it was a sport, and he would most definitely win gold.

Ryan's forehead rested against mine, and I could feel the steady and rapid beat of his heart against my chest. His hand gripped mine tightly against the door. I felt as if I were holding on, his grip the only anchor in the maelstrom of desire spinning me into its wake.

When Ryan held me and kissed me, I felt taken care of. Maybe that sounded weird, considering that I was also so turned on I could barely think past the need thrumming through my body. I could feel the slick heat between my thighs, and twinges of pleasure radiating outward. I distantly wondered if I could orgasm from nothing more than a kiss. I was already teetering on the edge of release, and I knew it wouldn't take much for me to fall over and shatter into pieces.

On the heels of a deep breath, I opened my eyes just as Ryan lifted his head. His deep blue gaze snagged mine instantly, and we stared at each other. The desire between us was a living, breathing force of its own. I could still feel it swirling through the currents in the air surrounding us.

The sound of him swallowing was audible before he took a step back. I instantly felt bereft and missed the heat of his strong body surrounding me. If my nipples could talk, they would've protested. Because that little tease of his thumb over my nipple—oh sweet hell, it was delicious.

The lines on Ryan's face were taut, his expression almost pained. The look in his eyes prompted me to ask, "Are you okay?"

My voice came out breathy. Seeing as I hadn't had a proper breath since he pressed me up against the door, I was *actually* breathless.

Ryan's face softened, and the low chuckle that followed sent a hot shiver through me, leaving me tingling all over.

"I suppose it depends on what you mean by okay. I want you. You said just one kiss, and you also told me we weren't having sex tonight."

The hand joined with mine slowly lowered, although he kept his fingers laced in mine as he took another step away. We were now linked just by our hands. His thumb began to move in slow circles along the edge of my wrist. My pulse thundered along as we stared at each other, and I tried to remember why I told him no sex.

Oh, right. With Ryan, it was easy to forget things. Which was strange for me. When it came to men, I was usually thinking way too much to relax. In the aftermath of my last relationship, a therapist had gently suggested that perhaps my need to be in control of my emotions contributed to my difficulty relaxing.

With Ryan, I simply surrendered to the moment. With him, I forgot to be tense when he kissed me and held me. I forgot to worry about what I should be doing, and if I was doing anything right. It all just happened, so fluidly that it made my knees weak and my insides feel funny.

"You said just one kiss," he repeated gently as his eyes searched my face. "I want to respect your boundaries." After a long moment, he spoke again. "Honestly, as much as I want you—and trust me, I want you—I don't want to ruin this by rushing it."

My heart did a funny little tumble, the heart equivalent of tripping and falling on its ass. "Oh," was all I could muster in reply.

"When can I take you out again?" he asked swiftly.

I bit my lip, literally trying to hold back the urge to say "tomorrow." Finally, the tiny voice of reason clamoring to be heard amongst the rushing roar of desire and need broke through. "I don't know. How about you text me?"

He nodded. His fingers slowly unlaced from mine. The moment his hand fell away, I wanted to snatch it back, to yank him to me for another kiss. But I needed to be sane here. I had set some boundaries for a reason.

Marshalling myself to stay strong, to contain the desire sliding like liquid fire through my veins, I took a breath and stepped away from the door. As if he somehow knew I needed the interruption, Barnable came trotting down the hallway, eyeing me expectantly.

"I should take him out and feed him," I said distractedly.

Ryan knelt down, holding his hand out when Barnable approached him. "You have a good night, little guy," he said as he scratched behind one of Barnable's ears.

When Ryan straightened again, his eyes landed on mine. My pulse immediately lunged to a gallop. Dear God. I *seriously* needed to get a grip around this man.

Curling my hand around the door knob, I opened it before I did something else stupid and impulsive. "Thank you for dinner. Good night," I said, my voice still breathy.

"Good night, Addie. I'll be in touch."

With that, Ryan left. Closing the heavy wooden door behind him, I leaned against it, resting my head back as I gulped in several deep breaths of air.

Chapter Thirteen

ADDIE

I adjusted my scarf and looked down at my feet. The toes of my familiar black leather cowboy boots looked back at me. I didn't often contemplate what other people thought of how I looked. Of all the things I was prone to worrying about, I felt blessed that for some reason, I had avoided that little curse.

That said, I was a tiny bit worried right now. The attorney, through Ryan's recommendation, had turned out to be lovely. He was an elderly man with a sly sense of humor and very thorough. He had turned over a letter in the estate paperwork that the former set of attorneys handling the estate had neglected to provide to me.

Among other things in the letter, Eleanor had given me the name of a personal friend and requested I stop by and check on her. So, here I was.

Trixie Canton lived a few blocks away from Eleanor's place in another brownstone on the Upper West Side. The door seemed gigantic and was painted bright purple. I liked that. The color gave me a dash of courage, so I lifted my hand and knocked.

I waited several moments before knocking again. As the time ticked past, I decided that perhaps Trixie wasn't home and turned to walk down the stairs. Just then, the door opened behind me, and I glanced back over my shoulder.

An elderly woman stood there, her white hair in a curly little halo around her head. She had a cane in one hand and wore a pair of pressed black slacks with a bright red blouse to match the red glasses perched on her nose.

Her eyes narrowed when she saw me. "Yes?" she asked in a clipped New York accent.

Turning, I fiddled with the end of my scarf. "Hello, I'm Addie Castille. My Aunt Eleanor left me a letter with your name and address, but no phone number, so I thought I'd stop by."

Trixie stared at me for a long moment and then rolled her eyes. "Oh, Ellie. Did she send you over to check on me?"

Considering that was precisely what the letter asked me to do, I told the truth. "Yes, she did."

Trixie's gaze softened slightly, and she smiled. "Come on in." Stepping back, she held the door open and gestured with her cane for me to pass through. After she closed the door, I followed her down a wide hallway with the sound of her cane tapping on the floor as she walked. "I don't get many visitors, so I'll just bring you into the kitchen if that's okay."

"Of course. I wouldn't have just dropped by like this, except Aunt Eleanor didn't leave a phone number, and I couldn't seem to find one for you."

"I have a phone, but it's still in my late husband's name. Bless his heart, he only died three years ago."

"I'm so sorry," I said, unsure what else to say about that.

"Thank you. He was ninety-seven. What can you expect? He lived a good life, and I figure that's the best blessing anyone can have before they die."

I followed Trixie into the kitchen. The

room had high ceilings with decorative moldings. Two tall windows looked out over a tiny courtyard outside. Trixie had a square table situated in front of the windows and pointed toward a chair for me to have a seat.

"Coffee or tea?" she asked as she walked slowly toward the counter.

"There's no need to make me anything."

Trixie clucked. "I already have coffee ready, dear, and it's no trouble to make tea."

"Coffee is fine. Thank you."

I unzipped my jacket and let it fall open as I unwound my scarf from around my neck. "Shall I help you get anything?" I called over.

Trixie waved her cane in the air as she turned. "Oh no. It's just one cup of coffee. I can certainly handle that."

In another moment, she handed me my coffee and pointed to the cream and sugar in the middle of the table. After she sat down across from me, she looked over, unabashedly eyeing me from head to toe.

"You must be Adelaide."

"I am. Did I forget to mention my name?" I paused to sip my coffee, which was delicious, rich, and dark.

"I'm not sure since my hearing isn't the best. I know Ellie was leaving everything to Adelaide. I presume that's you."

I smiled. "Did she mention she would be leaving me a letter suggesting I check in on you?"

"No, she didn't. Although we told each other just about everything, I doubt Ellie wanted me to know she might worry about me being alone after she died."

"Were you two close friends?"

"The very best," Trixie said firmly. "I miss her dearly. I'm not all alone though. My daughter comes by regularly. Enough about me. Tell me your plans for Eleanor's place."

"I'm going to stay there. I grew up in New Orleans, which you might know." Trixie nodded, so I continued, "When I learned I'd inherited Eleanor's place, I took it as a sign it was a good time to move."

"What did you do to your hand there?" she interjected, pointing to my hand.

I sighed. "My dog, Barnable, got lost the day after we got here. I was out looking for him one evening, and I heard him barking in return. Turns out, he got into someone's basement. I might have been accused of breaking and entering because I broke some glass to try to get to him."

Trixie burst out laughing. "Oh my. Did you get in trouble for that? Please tell me you've got Barnable back safe and sound."

"Barnable is fine, and I managed not to get arrested. I just cut my hand."

"Do you happen to know where he was?"

"Yes. The owner of the home was Ryan Blake."

Trixie's eyes widened as her brows hitched up. "Oh my word. Your dog managed to break into the home of one of the wealthiest men in the neighborhood. How in the world did you keep him from calling the police?"

"I just told him the truth." I shrugged. "Considering that Barnable *was* in his basement barking, he seemed to believe me. He's actually ended up being quite nice. I even went on a dinner date with him."

Trixie laughed again. "Well, well. Ryan Blake's beating models off with a stick, and he takes you out to dinner. Don't get me wrong. You're a lovely girl. It's just he's known for not getting personal."

"So I gathered. I actually looked him up online," I admitted.

Trixie chuckled before pausing to take a sip from her coffee. "I'm guessing you saw some things about his family."

"Just a bit. I was curious after meeting him."

Trixie laughed again. "It's no secret he

had a terrible falling out with his father, and his brother's death was so sad. It's always terrible when people die young. Rumor had it, his father even tried to cut Ryan out of the will, but he couldn't because the company was originally founded by his maternal grandfather."

"I saw that in the news, but I wasn't sure it was true."

"Oh yes. Despite Ryan's reputation for being a bit cold when it comes to women, I always found him to be quite the gentleman. He doesn't seem to think much of social expectations. Considering I think they're bullshit too, that works for me."

"Do you mind me asking how you know him?"

"My husband knew Ryan peripherally through business. They were decades apart in age and weren't friends, but I met Ryan at a charity function. Ryan's also on the board of a dog rescue program with me."

I sputtered on my sip of coffee. One of Trixie's silver brows arched up as she cast me a smile. I reached for the napkin she handed over from the center of her kitchen table. "Surprised?" she queried.

"Yes," I said after I dabbed at my mouth and wiped up the drops of coffee on her table. "Although I did read he was rumored to be a donor for an animal shelter, so I suppose that's true."

Trixie shrugged lightly. "Ryan doesn't say much about it, but then he doesn't say much about anything personal. He still lives in the house where he grew up. His soft spot for animals is probably why he didn't call the police on you."

"How very interesting," I finally said. At that moment, the doorbell rang in her house. "Do you need me to get that for you?"

"Oh no. It's my daughter. I'd love for you to meet her."

I heard the door opening and a voice calling, "Hi, Mom!"

Footsteps approached down the echoing hallway, and a woman who looked to be about my mother's age walked into the kitchen. She had blond hair pulled up in a ponytail and bright blue eyes behind a pair of glasses. Her smile was wide and welcoming.

"I didn't know you had company, Mom," Trixie's daughter said as she approached the table. She held out her hand. "I'm Tara."

I stood from the table. "Hi, I'm Addie."

"This is Ellie's great-niece," Trixie said. "Help yourself to some coffee and join us."

"So nice to meet you, Addie," Tara called

over her shoulder as she walked across the kitchen to pour some coffee.

"Nice to meet you as well," I replied before sitting back down in my chair.

Tara turned back with her coffee. She sat down at an angle across from me. "So, you're Ellie's great-niece? She told us all about you."

"You know, I'm so grateful that she left me basically everything, but I can't say I knew her well. I grew up in New Orleans with my family. She got married and moved away. I came up to visit with my mother once when I was a little girl. I sent holiday and birthday cards every year though. Apparently, I'm the only one who did that."

Trixie grinned and tapped her cane on the floor. "Ellie was delighted with your cards every year. They were so creative."

I laughed. "Oh yes, I really got into my cards and made them all by myself when I was little. It turned into a career. I design cards for a greeting card company. It pays rather well, and I can work wherever I want. It made it easy for me to move here."

"What a cool job," Tara said with a smile.

"Addie went out on a dinner date with Ryan Blake," Trixie interjected with a twinkle in her eye.

Tara's eyes widened. "Really?"

"Really." I quickly recounted the story of how I met Ryan and our dinner date. "He's been quite nice," I finished. I completely left out our two heated kisses. I wasn't ready to dive into that.

"Be careful, my mother's going to try to matchmake," Tara warned.

"I don't need to matchmake. He already took her out for dinner. I believe it's true love," Trixie teased.

A bit later, I walked down the steps as I left Trixie's place, smiling inside and out. Although I'd wanted to move to New York City and was looking forward to the adventure of an entirely different place, I missed my friends and family dearly. Aside from Ryan, few people had even bothered to say hello. I didn't sense New Yorkers were an unfriendly sort, just not quite as forthcoming as Southerners were in saying hello to strangers. Meeting my great aunt's closest friend and her daughter made me feel as if I had a little circle of belonging in this big city.

A gust of wind blew down the street, and I looked upward into the slate gray sky. I was impatient for it to snow and looking forward to seeing the city dusted in white. I felt the vibration of my phone as I walked down the steps into the subway. I was feeling on top of it because I'd mastered the logistics of getting on and off the subway.

Once I was seated, I slipped my phone out of my pocket and glanced at the screen.

Sexy Suit: *Dinner tonight?*

I couldn't help it. My lips tugged into a smile, and my heart did a little tumble in my chest while butterflies set flight in my belly.

That was how bad I had it for Ryan Blake. I needed to stop thinking like this. I didn't need to get ahead of myself and fall for some guy who treated romance more like business as far as his reputation indicated.

But what if he really likes you? My ever so hopeful heart whispered.

Staring at the screen, I contemplated how to answer his text.

Chapter Fourteen

RYAN

"Tonight?"

I spun in my desk chair to look out over the Manhattan skyline.

"Yes, tonight," Graham replied in my ear.

I adjusted my cell phone in my hand. "Fuck. I forgot all about it."

"Need to rustle up one of your dates?" Graham's tone was slightly sarcastic.

"Nah. I'll fly solo. I'm not up for trying to find a date tonight."

Graham chuckled in my ear. "Not so sure that's a smart move. You showing up solo means there will be questions. Should I ask Soraya if she's got a friend who might want to go?"

"For God's sake, no. I'll find my own date."

"All right, then. We'll see you there. We're seated at the same table, so at least we can have a decent conversation."

"Thank fuck for that."

After I hung up, I stared at Addie's last text. She'd turned me down for dinner last night. I wondered what I would need to say to get a yes from her. I didn't let myself think too hard.

Sexy Suit: *Here's the thing. I need a date for a charity function tonight. You're the only person I want to take. I promise just one kiss. If you don't even want that, then no kisses.*

I hit send and set my phone on my desk as I stood from my chair, sliding my hands into my pockets. I had tossed my suit jacket off hours ago. Today has been a day of meeting upon meeting in the morning and hours scouring numbers this afternoon.

I'd never shied away from hard work. I'd busted my fucking ass to turn around my grandfather's company. My father had been an entitled prick who almost ran it into the ground with his selfish decisions.

I stared out past the skyline of Manhattan, and idly wondered what it would be like to seriously consider a relationship. To say my parents' marriage had been awful was an understatement. They basically hated each other. My father married my mother for her money, and she ended up resenting him deeply for convincing her otherwise at the beginning.

Colin and I bonded tightly as brothers. We were each other's only support in the miserable household of our family. My mind spun to a memory.

George's claws clicked on the floor as I closed the front door behind me and let my backpack slide off my shoulder. "Hey George," I said as I plunked down on the floor beside him and petted him while he licked my face. George was the brightest spot in my life. He was an amiable black lab mix given to Colin and me by our aunt.

"Hello there, Ryan," Hazel said as she walked down the hallway.

Hazel was my father's assistant and often ran interference between him and everyone else. I looked up at her. "Hi."

"Your father's working in his study this afternoon."

That was all she needed to say. I scrambled to my feet and snatched my backpack up. I started to run up the stairs, but I caught myself in time and slowed to the fastest walk I could manage without making much noise. After I crested the top stair, I kept at my pace until I reached my bedroom door, turning the knob and pushing through.

Once inside the privacy of my own room, I sank my hips onto my bed and dropped my backpack at my feet. I scrubbed my face with my hands and wished my father had stayed at the office. Whenever he was home, it was an exercise in avoidance.

Standing, I pulled my books out of my backpack and walked to my desk. I might as well get my homework done.

There was a soft scratching sound at my door. A smile tugged at my lips because George had followed me upstairs. Forgetting my father was home for a moment, I ran across my room to open the door.

George came bounding in. Just as I was about to shut the door behind him, my father's voice reached me. "How many times do I have to tell you to keep that dog quiet?"

I closed my eyes and took a breath as anger hit me hard, tightening like a cold fist in my chest. There were so many things I wanted to say. All I said was, "Sorry, father."

I waited to see if he said anything else before I closed the door. A full minute or more ticked by while my heart pounded in my ears, and I felt sick and angry.

I finally closed my door and hoped he wouldn't

come and open it. Every single moment with my father was spent tiptoeing. He occasionally exploded, but that was almost a relief from the relentless cold, cruel way he treated everyone in the family. People simply existing in his world were an annoyance for him.

The sound of my phone chiming on my desk nudged me out of that memory. I snagged my phone off my desk to see a return text from Addie. Before I even finished reading it, I was smiling.

Well, when you put it like that, how can I say no? What is this function, and what should I wear?

My smile stretched wide, and the unfamiliar sensation of joy flashed through me.

I quickly tapped out my reply.

It's a fundraiser for an animal rescue program. Sadly, it's a formal function. Can you swing that?

Her reply was swift. *Of course I can, Sexy Suit. I'll blow your mind.*

I was laughing as I replied. *Can I pick you up at six?*

Yes, sir.

Any rules I should know about? I queried. I didn't specify kisses, but that's what I meant.

I waited for her next reply with my heart kicking hard and fast against my ribs. To say I was unaccustomed to this kind of reaction to a woman didn't even come close to capturing how I felt about Addie. She actually made me nervous, something I hadn't felt in many years. She also elicited a sense of hope, like a plant shimmying up through a crack in the barren desert of my heart.

Hmmm... Came her next text.

I patiently waited for what might come next, turning to stare out the windows with my phone in hand. There I was, a lovesick boy, waiting for some girl to text me back. Even stranger than all of it was the fact I didn't even care. Not about the way I felt about Addie. I just wanted the next few hours to fly by so I could pick her up. My phone vibrated in my hand, and my eyes whipped downward to look at the screen.

More than one kiss.

I feel like I won something.

Don't congratulate yourself too soon.

I got a wink emoticon at the end of that.

Point taken. I'll see you at six.

Chapter Fifteen

RYAN

Hours later, I knocked on Addie's door. It turned out that simply being honest got me to that yes. I needed a date because Graham was right. Flying solo at a social event like this would only end up being more of a headache than it was worth.

Standing in front of Addie's door, I took a breath and shifted my shoulders slightly. This was a black-tie event, and it was chilly tonight, so I had a wool overcoat on. Snow was falling lightly from the sky.

I heard Barnable's low-throated bark and smiled to myself. In another moment, the doorknob turned, and Addie opened it. She literally took my breath away.

"Come in," she said, gesturing me inside as Barnable circled my feet.

I gave my head a shake to keep from gaping at her and stepped inside. A gust of cold air came in with me before Addie shut the door.

"You look stunning," I said simply.

Her cheeks flushed. "Well, thank you. I told you I could pull this off. You seem shocked. Did you doubt me?" she teased.

"Not for one second."

Her cheeks flushed a deeper shade of pink, and she turned away to fetch her coat hanging on the coat rack by the door. Her silky dress wasn't particularly revealing, yet she was a vision of temptation. The top was slightly fitted around her waist with the sleeves coming down to her elbows before flaring out in a subtle ruffle. The skirt also flared out at her knees, twirling when she moved. The soft cream color set off the rich amber of her skin, and she looked downright edible. She wore a pair of fitted boots that hugged her calves. Addie somehow looked modern and retro at once. She was definitely a woman who had style, and yet, it all seemed natural, rather than an elaborate calculation.

Addie shrugged into a long wool coat,

buttoning it quickly as she turned to face me again. "Are we taking the subway?"

"No. I have a driver."

Addie rolled her eyes at that. "Of course you do."

I shrugged. "Make fun if you like. I don't use my driver all the time, but it's cold out, and it's starting to snow."

Addie squealed. "Really?"

"Yes. Is this exciting?"

"I've never actually seen snow. Not outside of photos."

She knelt down and stroked her hand over Barnable's head. "You be a good boy. I'll be back in a few hours."

When we stepped outside, Addie came to an abrupt stop when I closed the door behind us. With her hands clasped in front of her chest, she looked up into the snow as it fell lazily from the sky. The fluffy snowflakes glittered as they passed through the light cast by the streetlights. Addie turned to look at me, the joy evident on her face with her beaming smile.

"Snow," she said, her tone a reverent whisper.

The part of me that was cynical and sarcastic almost spoke up to point out that it might not seem so amazing after the grit and grime of New York streets got a hold of it. Yet, snow was magical when it was clean and covering the city like light fairy dust.

My hopeful self, a side of myself I really didn't know very well, held sway over my tendency toward sarcasm. "It's beautiful, isn't it?"

I waited beside her as she stared up into the sky. After a moment, she looked back at me. "It is. Okay, I'm ready."

"There will be more snow this winter. I promise."

After she locked the door, I took her hand and led her down the steps to my car waiting at the curb. Although I did have a driver, Smitty knew I had no patience with him getting the door for me, or anyone else.

Once Addie was seated, I rounded the car and slid into the opposite side and closed the door. I gestured to the front. "Addie, this is Smitty. If you need anything, just let him know."

"Very nice to meet you, miss," Smitty said, glancing over his shoulder with a wink. Smitty was going on eighty and still flirted like a teenage boy.

Addie cast him a wide smile. "So nice to meet you."

With a nod, Smitty began driving. He

took up an easy conversation with Addie as he made his way through downtown Manhattan. It didn't surprise me in the slightest to discover Addie had a million or more questions about New York City, all of which Smitty was happy to expound upon.

After he pulled up to the curb in front of the arts hall, he glanced back and looked from Addie to me. "You're a lucky man," he said with a sly grin.

"I'm aware of that."

Chapter Sixteen

ADDIE

The hum of voices was constant, mingling with the sound of glasses and silverware clicking. Ryan sat beside me, taking a swallow of his scotch as he chuckled at something one of the other guests at the table said

Soraya leaned over to murmur in my ear. "These things can be a bit much. How are you doing?"

I liked Soraya. She was sharp and funny and didn't seem to care much for trying to fit in. With her dark hair and striking looks, she was a stunner. She also took no bullshit and teased her husband, Graham, with abandon.

"I'm doing fine. I might seem like a fish out of water, but I can handle myself."

Soraya leaned back in her chair and took a sip of her wine. "I like you. I think you're going to be good for Ryan."

Her eyes bounced from me to him. "Ryan, I sure hope you have enough sense to keep Addie."

Ryan's warm gaze caught mine before he looked back at Soraya. "I like to consider myself an intelligent man," he teased.

Graham chuckled. "Looks like you might have to prove it to my wife."

Ryan slid his arm around my shoulders. The feel of his warm palm landing between my shoulder blades was like a hot brand. Heat twisted in my core. "I'm up for the challenge," he said. When he looked toward me, his gaze was dead serious, and I was suddenly flustered.

Soraya seemed to sense my stress and replied lightly, "Do your best."

Someone stopped by the table, one of many people who wanted to talk to Ryan and Graham about business, and the conversation moved along. As the evening wore on, what little I had allowed myself to read about Ryan was proved to be true. He was socially sought after, and plenty of women seemed more than a little curious about who I was and why he was with me.

The benefit was an art auction to raise money for an animal shelter. At one point during the bidding, a woman all but stole Ryan from my side, dragging him off to talk to him about something.

Soraya muttered something under her breath, and I looked to her. "Excuse me?"

"That's Crystal Stokes. She's had her eye on Ryan forever. He took her to one function like this, and never again after that."

Glancing to Soraya, I said, "He's only taken me out twice. It's not like I can read anything into that."

Soraya arched one of her dark brows. "Ryan likes you. Graham even thinks so."

My cheeks heated, and I shrugged slightly. "Maybe."

Graham came over, sliding his arm around Soraya's waist. His hand curled over her hip possessively as he leaned down to press a kiss on her cheek. "How much longer do we need to stay?" he asked.

"I'm not leaving Addie here alone," Soraya replied swiftly. "Some of the people here are the human equivalent of sharks."

Graham's eyes shifted to me, and he smiled indulgently. "Pretty sure Addie can handle it on her own. Plus, she's got Ryan."

"Not with Crystal trying to get her claws

into him. Go get him back over here," she ordered, nudging Graham with her elbow.

Not that I had any doubt about Graham's obvious adoration of Soraya, but he further proved the point by not even hesitating. He strolled over and promptly cut into the conversation, which appeared mostly one-sided on Crystal's part. In another moment, he was walking back towards us with Ryan.

"As you wish," he said when he stopped beside Soraya again. He caught her hand in his and lifted it to dust a kiss over her knuckles.

"Sorry about that," Ryan said as he stopped at my side.

"You don't have to stay beside me the entire night."

"I know I don't," he murmured. "But I'd rather. That was a distraction and a complete waste of my time."

Glancing up at him, I noticed the lines of tension on his face and irritation flashing in his eyes. Whatever Crystal had wanted to discuss didn't appear to be sitting well with him.

Graham and Soraya were drawn away from us by another business associate, and Ryan looked down, turning to face me. He was downright dashing. With his dark hair and glacial blue eyes, his black and white suit set off the contrast.

"Thank you for coming tonight," he said, the gravelly sound of his voice sending goose-bumps prickling over my skin as I looked up into his eyes.

"Of course," I managed to reply, my own voice coming out raspy.

He reached for my hand, catching it in his. "How's your other hand feeling?"

When his thumb began to brush back and forth right along the sensitive area on the inside of my wrist, it felt as if fire was licking across the surface of my skin, radiating away from his touch. I had to force myself to focus and almost forgot what his original question was.

"It's fine." I lifted my other hand between us, twisting it to the side so he could see. "The stitches are already absorbing, and there's no more redness. See?"

He glanced down and looked carefully before I lowered my arm. "I do. Daniel did a nice job with those stitches. I'm guessing the scars won't be too bad."

I bit my lip. "He did. Thank you again for calling him that night. I haven't had a chance to tell that story to many people, but everyone seems a little surprised you didn't call the police on me."

Ryan's low chuckle warmed me, spinning around my heart like a lasso.

"I almost did. But once you explained..." He paused, shrugging his shoulders. "I knew you were telling the truth, so I didn't see any reason to call the police."

His thumb kept teasing the skin on my wrist, and I felt a flush break out along with goosebumps. Heat suffused me. When Ryan was focusing his attention on me like this, it felt as if we were all alone in the world. The people and noise around us receded into the background.

Impulsively, I leaned up and brushed my lips across his. A little shock passed through my body at the point of contact.

"Don't you dare tell me that's my one kiss," he murmured.

"I didn't say only one kiss."

My belly felt funny, and I was tingling all over, a sense of joy fizzing in my veins.

"No, you didn't. But I was fully prepared for you to set a limit."

Although desire had overridden most of my common sense, I was dimly aware we were in a very public location. Without that awareness, I probably would've flung myself into his arms and wound myself around him like a vine.

With his searing gaze on mine, I shook my head. "More than one."

Chapter Seventeen

ADDIE

It felt like hours and hours by the time we left the function. Ryan didn't leave my side for the rest of the evening. Although much of the night involved being polite and smiling and nodding along as various people sought Ryan's attention, I enjoyed myself. For one, I did love to dress up. But more than that, I enjoyed being with Ryan.

I couldn't say what I'd expected, but I certainly hadn't expected Ryan to be so attentive, and so focused on my needs. Considering this was a fundraiser for a charity, and apparently he was one of their largest donors, it wasn't as if he could blow off his other responsibilities. Yet somehow, he managed to make me feel as if I were the center of his attention even when he was talking to others.

He either had his hand on my back, coaxing me in whatever direction we needed to go, or he had my hand clasped in his firm grip. I managed not to drink too much champagne, but I had just enough to take the edge off of my nervousness.

It was also a boon that the charity in question was something I genuinely felt passionate about. With Barnable a rescue, and my awareness of the acute problems faced with animal shelters being overcrowded in so many areas, I could actually talk about the issue without difficulty. While some teased that getting a rescue was a form of virtue signaling, I called bullshit on that.

There were far too many animals who needed a home, and I was happy to get behind the cause. I recalled Trixie's comments about how she knew Ryan through their work on this board together, and I couldn't help but wonder a bit about it. Ryan kept quiet about his involvement and simply played the role of another businessman showing his face at a society function and donating money.

"I think we're clear to leave." The feel of Ryan's gruff whisper as he leaned close to my ear once again sent goosebumps prickling down that entire side of my body. My heart did a little pitter-pat, and my belly executed a quick flip when I looked up into his eyes.

"We are?"

"If we don't leave soon, I'm likely to kiss you senseless and take that dress off you right here in the middle of this ballroom."

I sputtered a cough as my eyes widened. "Okay then. I'm ready whenever you are."

Ryan had such a powerful effect on me. He scrambled my usual sassy, teasing attitude, forcing me to reach for it so I didn't look too much the fool. As he escorted me out of the room with his hand warm on my back, sending heat radiating in spirals through my entire body, he slipped his phone out and made a quick call.

"Smitty, meet us out front. We should be on the sidewalk in just a few minutes." He nodded in reply to whatever Smitty said on the other end before slipping his phone back in the inner pocket of his jacket.

"Thank you again for coming tonight," he said as we moved through the cluster of people in front of the doors.

Glancing up, I replied, "Of course. I did tell you we would have dinner again."

Ryan stopped, his long stride pausing. As

his eyes searched my face, he said no more before he resumed walking. He raised his hand as we paused near the coat check, and in another moment, he was holding my jacket for me to slide my arms in. After the jacket settled on my shoulders, I felt his hands squeeze lightly before he leaned down and dusted two hot kisses on the back of my neck.

Each kiss felt like a drop of hot lava on my skin. Sparks skittered outward, as electricity sizzled down my spine. My knees actually felt weak, and all he'd done was barely kiss the back of my neck. I was in so far over my head it wasn't even funny.

Someone's elbow bumped me as they walked by, and Ryan straightened. He shifted to stand on my other side, effectively shielding me from the crowd bustling around us as he shrugged into his own jacket.

His gaze swept over my face. "You okay?"

"I'm fine. It's crowded, and somebody bumped into me. No big deal."

I swear, the man almost growled when we were jostled again.

"I'm sure Smitty is waiting," I added.

Ryan let out a laugh under his breath and slid his arm around my shoulders. "I'm sure. Let's not make him wait too long."

In another moment, he was holding the door open for me. The cool winter air was a balm to the heat building inside of me as we stepped out of the crush of people and into the winter night.

"The snow stopped," I said as I looked up toward the sky.

"I thought it would," Ryan replied.

He was already guiding me through the people crowded on the stairs. In another moment, he was holding the car door as I slid into the backseat. The car was an understated black sedan. I didn't doubt it was luxurious, but it certainly wasn't showy. If anything, I'd guess Ryan preferred it to be as low profile as possible.

"To Ms. Castille's place?" Smitty asked with a glance at us in the backseat once Ryan had closed the door on his side.

"Please. Straight there." Ryan slid his gaze to mine in the semi-darkness. "Unless you have a request."

I shook my head. "No, thank you. Home is perfect."

At that, Smitty tapped a button and the divider between the front and the back rolled up. I didn't know how to describe what happened in the seconds that followed except to say it felt as if a match was lit. The thrumming of desire that flashed to life the moment Ryan and I were alone in the backseat was like flint to stone.

The space felt tiny and crowded by the desire racing through me. And yet, when I looked across the seat toward Ryan, the space between us felt immense, a chasm so great I almost feared to cross it.

The crucible of our attraction rose before me. I'd never felt a need so great. It felt as if my entire body was filled with sparks colliding with each other and creating more heat. Fire spun through my veins, and my arousal was slick between my thighs.

All we were doing was sitting there. The car hadn't even pulled away from the curb yet. There was a crush of traffic on the street, and I distantly heard the sound of the blinker clicking from the front of the car.

The silence between us was heavy, weighted with an intensity I'd never experienced. When my eyes met Ryan's in the shadows, I knew he wasn't going to make a move. It was on me to act on the need spinning like a storm inside of me.

With blood rushing through my ears with every resounding beat of my heart and my breath coming in shallow pants, I reached across the seat between us, the leather cool under my palm.

Ryan's hand curled over mine, and he watched me quietly. He gave such a subtle tug I wouldn't have recognized it if I weren't so hyper-aware of everything in this moment, most particularly him. I uncrossed my legs. The sound from the silk of my dress was audible as fabric shifted.

"Come here." Those two words fell from Ryan's lips in a gravelly but soft command, like velvet spun over steel to soften the power behind the words.

There was no question I would grant his request. I wouldn't quite call it an order, but his words appealed to the primal desire rushing through me.

He exerted no further pressure on my hand. I tried to corral the storm spinning inside of me, but I couldn't. So, I did the only thing I could. I turned toward him and slid across the seat until my thigh bumped against his. Then, everything happened so fast.

Ryan released my hand, his palm sliding up my spine to angle me in his direction. With his other hand lacing into my hair, he whispered my name right before his lips crashed into mine.

There was nothing graceful or measured about this kiss. It was as if we clasped hands and jumped from a plane together. We were spinning with nothing to anchor us as we held onto each other. With our mouths fused, and our tongues tangling, we let the storm of need tug us right into its center.

I lost all sense of time and place, savoring the strength of Ryan as he pulled me into his lap. My knees straddled his hips with my dress sliding up my thighs. I let out a satisfied moan at the feel of his arousal pressing against my core.

Ryan abruptly tore his lips from mine, his head leaning back against the seat with a pained growl. It was then I noticed the car slowing, and heard the sound of the blinker again.

"You've ruined me, Addie," he said flatly as he lifted his head, his eyes piercing mine.

Barely able to catch my breath, I stared back at him, acutely aware of the hot press of his length against me. The car slowed and came to a stop.

"We're here," he murmured. "Let me walk you up."

I heard the sound of the divider between the front and back begin to move, and I scrambled off Ryan's lap. By the time Smitty turned to glance over his shoulder, I hoped the darkness hid how unsettled I was.

"I'll walk home from here," Ryan said.

I barely heard Smitty's comment and managed to tell him good night. Moments later, we walked up my front steps. The sound of the door clicking shut behind us echoed through my body. I was attuned to everything.

Sensations were still spinning through me from our heated kiss in the car, and it felt as if my nerve endings were on fire. I glanced up toward Ryan, and my breath caught in my throat. I couldn't exactly say my pulse had slowed down much, but it instantly raced again.

His eyes searched my face. After a long moment, while my heart beat madly inside my chest, he asked, "Shall I go then?"

"No." That single word slipped out in a raspy whisper.

Just then, the sound of Barnable's claws clicking on the hardwood floor alerted us to his presence. Ryan spoke first. "Hey there, buddy," he said, dropping his hand from where it had been resting on my back when he knelt down to greet Barnable with a few scratches behind his ears.

Considering that my dog was my very

best friend, and I was one of those people who measured the quality of others by their kindness to animals, it said something that my disappointment at the loss of Ryan's touch overrode the fact that I was pleased Barnable liked him.

With a mental shake, I leaned over, trailing my fingertips over Barnable's back and murmuring a greeting as Ryan straightened.

Satisfied that we both greeted him, Barnable turned and trotted back down the hallway. Now that he was comfortable in the house, his preferred napping spot was on the dog bed in the kitchen.

Ryan and I stood in the entryway. I turned to face him again. "Would you like something to drink?" I asked because it was the only thing I could think to say.

Ryan held my gaze as heat radiated from my core, suffusing my entire body. He shook his head slowly. "There's only one thing I want."

His tone held a promise—a naughty, dirty promise.

"What's that?" I heard myself whispering.

He stepped closer, lifting a hand to tuck my hair behind my ear, his fingers sliding into the strands as he cupped the back of my neck. "This."

That single word was like a match dropping into the kindling of desire between us. His lips brushed across mine, and we tumbled back into another hot, deep, and overwhelming kiss. We picked up right where we left off in the car.

Except this time, there was nothing to interrupt us, nothing to calm the storm.

By the time awareness flickered, my back was against the wall by the stairs, and every inch of Ryan's hard, muscled body was pressed against me as he devoured my mouth.

My head fell back against the wall as I gulped in deep mouthfuls of air. I was hot all over and so driven by need I could barely tolerate it. Opening my eyes, I found his intense gaze waiting.

Without thinking, I reached for his hand where it was pressed against the wall beside my shoulder. Lacing my fingers into his, I turned and led him up the stairs. I didn't know where I meant for this to go, but I knew it couldn't stop now.

Chapter Eighteen

RYAN

I didn't even know how we got there, but I found myself standing at the foot of Addie's bed with her dark eyes pinned on mine.

She had this ridiculously tall bed. At the moment, she was sitting on it with her dress rumpled around her hips. Her index finger curled around my belt, and she pulled me toward her.

"Kiss me again," she said her words a husky command that I had no choice but to obey.

Kissing Addie was pure heaven. Her soft, plush lips were mobile, and her tongue was a sensuous tease. When I stepped into the cradle of her hips, I could feel the heat of her core against my achingly hard cock. I cupped one of her breasts in my palm, savoring the little hitch in her throat as I teased her nipple to a tight, ruched peak through the silk of her dress.

Usually, I was in control when it came to women and sex. Sex was often a calculated interaction. Nothing, *absolutely* nothing, with Addie was calculated. Trying to restrain the lust driving me was like trying to hold a storm at bay with my own hands.

My palm slid up her thigh, and I couldn't hold back a low growl when I reached the top of her stockings and felt her silky bare skin. I should've known she was the kind of woman who actually wore a garter with her stockings.

I didn't know how it was even possible, but another shot of blood swelled my cock even further. I dropped a hot trail of kisses down the side of her neck, delighting in the sweet tang of her skin.

Addie's hips shifted, and a soft moan escaped. "Ryan," she gasped as I teased my fingers over the silk between her thighs. Satisfaction jolted through me to find the silk was drenched. Considering I was hanging on to my control by a frayed thread, it was a relief to discover perhaps she was as deeply affected.

Her hips bucked into my hand, and she gasped my name again, this time her tone bordering on angry. Lifting my head reluctantly, I paused to look at her. With her breasts rising and falling rapidly with every breath, I could see the wild beat of her pulse in her neck. Her dark hair fell in a glossy tumble around her shoulders, and her lips were swollen and pink from our kisses.

"Yes?" I murmured as I took a moment to lightly squeeze one of her nipples.

Her eyes opened, her gaze heavy-lidded as she stared at me with desire and a hint of annoyance flashing in the dark depths. "You're teasing me," she gasped just as I stroked my fingers over that damp silk between her thighs again.

"So?"

Addie's eyes flashed again right before she shifted and reached between us to drag her palm brazenly over the hard ridge of my cock. My breath hissed between my teeth.

Much as I wanted to be buried deep in the heart of her, there was a part of myself— one I admittedly didn't recognize—that didn't want to rush this, that wanted to savor Addie for the gift she was.

"Let me take care of you," I whispered.

As we stared at each other in the dim

lighting of the bedroom, I saw something flicker deep in her gaze, a hint of vulnerability and surprise. Addie's teeth sank into her bottom lip as I hooked a finger over the edge of her silk panties and teased into her slick folds. As I watched, she dipped her chin slightly. Although she didn't say a word, somehow I knew that was her acknowledgment of my request.

I wanted to watch her fly apart. I dipped my head briefly to dust hot kisses along the neckline of her dress, pausing for a moment with a last kiss right where the silk dipped down to a V in the valley between her breasts. I lingered for a moment, breathing in her scent and loving the subtle arch of her body into mine.

I *finally* sank a finger knuckle deep into her core. She cried out sharply, her entire body tensing as her hips arched to meet the motion of my hand. Another finger joined the first, stretching into her tight, silken channel.

I watched as her eyes fell closed, her body arching and flexing as I slowly fucked her with my fingers. I'd never in my life gloried in the pleasure of a woman the way I did Addie's at this moment.

I waited, savoring every little sound that

fell from her lips. When her channel pulsed around my fingers and her scent drifted to me, I gave in and leaned down to let my mouth join the action.

Addie's sharp cry was pure pleasure. She tasted tangy and sweet, and I loved how she rocked into every stroke of my tongue as my fingers pressed deeper and deeper. I only teased my tongue in a circle around her clit when I felt her channel begin to ripple around my fingers. She cried out roughly, her hands falling back on the bed as she climaxed.

I felt as if I had run a marathon simply through the act of bringing her to her release. I was beyond the point of aching with need for her. Yet, I was determined not to give in. Not tonight.

No matter what, Addie would know I wasn't in this solely to meet my own needs. My heart was thrashing in my chest, its beat a drum of recognition of just how much I wanted her. I straightened, wrestling to quell the need tying me up in knots.

When Addie's eyes slowly opened, immediately catching mine, everything stopped for a moment. An intense emotion gripped me, a mix of what I could only imagine might be love and an intense protectiveness. I didn't quite think I was in love with Addie just yet, but I knew I wanted her more than I'd ever wanted anyone.

She shifted forward, reaching for my belt. "Your turn."

Chapter Nineteen

ADDIE

Ryan's hand curled around my wrist, his grip gentle but firm. "Not tonight," he murmured, his voice gruff and taut.

With the tremors of my climax still echoing through my body, I lifted my eyes to his face. Perhaps I had misread what I thought was his reciprocal desire. The searing heat was still there in his eyes. The blue had gone so dark it was almost navy. My eyes dropped again to the outline of his cock in his slacks.

Lifting my gaze again, I asked, "Why?"

When I dropped my hand, he released it easily and rested both of his beside my hips on the bed. Given that he had just sent me flying with one of the most intense orgasms

I'd ever had, I was shocked to feel my pulse pick up its pace again.

The mattress dipped under his weight, and a shiver chased over my skin at the look in his eyes and the way it felt to have his strength surrounding me. "Because I want to wait."

"But why?"

"This isn't a one-time thing for me. It's important to me that you don't think that it is."

My heart skipped a beat, and I felt cracked wide open as if he could see all the insecurities I carried inside. I took a breath, trying to marshal myself together. The thing was, the raw need I felt for Ryan was so fierce, it was hard to think. All I knew was who and what I wanted.

"I promise I won't think all you want is a one night stand," I said quickly.

Ryan dropped his head with a low chuckle. His forehead rested against my shoulder before he turned and pressed a hot kiss on the sensitive skin where my neck met my shoulder.

That kiss was like a lick of fire. He lifted his head, his eyes earnest as he looked at me. "Don't confuse this for thinking I don't want you. Oh, I want you. Like I've never wanted anyone in my life. But my reputation precedes me, and I know it. It's not just about tonight. I want you to give me a real chance."

I had absolutely no idea what to make of this. Ryan's reputation did precede him. It wasn't that he was a player. He simply treated his dating life more like a business with benefits arrangement.

Meanwhile, my heart was going a little crazy, doing cartwheels inside my chest. Trust came to me easily in some ways—with new friendships, or when the universe sent my life along a different path.

Yet, there was one glaring exception to my natural inclination to trust in the universe and be open to what the world offered me. It all revolved around men and my heart. I hadn't had my own heart broken by some asshole. No, I had my heart broken a piece at a time watching while my mother longed for my father, a man who was never there for her, or for me.

Ryan couldn't have known just how much he was like my father. My father was wealthy. He had a cold and distant relationship with everyone in his family, including me, his only daughter. He'd met my mother when she was young and impressionable. I suppose one distinction between my father and Ryan was that my father enjoyed stringing women along for nothing more than fun. When he tired of them, he cast them aside. He tired of my mother once her pregnancy became visible.

She was his only marriage, and it had been short-lived. I adored my family and felt loved to pieces, but my *family* was limited to the maternal side for me. My father's family was a void of nothing.

My childhood had been a series of tiny heartbreaks. I gradually came to a sense of acceptance about the reality of my father, that he would never be there for me, or for my mother. Although I was by nature a cheerful, optimistic person, I was cynical when it came to romance. I had no hopes for it, and I spent years promising myself I would never end up like my mother. For most of her adult life, she'd longed for a man who never intended to be there in any meaningful way.

Ryan had absolutely no idea how many buttons of mine he was pushing. Actually, it was just one gigantic red button, like one of those emergency buttons at a nuclear power plant. To have him here telling me he wanted me to take him seriously was almost laughably ridiculous.

And evidently, I hadn't done as thorough a job as I'd thought of silencing the wishful voice in my heart. It might be hoarse and barely audible because I'd all but cut its vocal cords, but that wishful voice still managed to cry out now in protest of the rest of me.

I stared at Ryan, feeling far more vulnerable than I'd ever wanted to feel. "I don't understand," I finally said. I absolutely did *not* understand.

Ryan was quiet as his eyes searched my face. With my heartbeat thudding in my ears, I felt as if I were waiting on the edge of a precipice.

"I'm not sure I do either," he replied slowly, his low gravelly voice sending another prickle of goosebumps over my skin. My desire for this man just wouldn't quit. "All I know is I want you, and I like you. A lot."

He leaned forward once more and caught my lips in a lingering kiss. There was nothing naughty about that kiss, nothing dirty. It felt almost chaste, and yet so intimate my belly filled with butterflies and my heart practically beat its way out of my chest.

He drew away slowly, and his lashes brushed against his cheeks when he looked down. The sound of his swallow was audible in the quiet room. "Fuck me. Stockings? You actually wear stockings with a garter." His eyes lifted to mine, the look there almost pained. "You're going to kill me."

"I wasn't hoping to kill you. I was just hoping you might fuck me."

Ryan let out a choked laugh at that. In a few quick, efficient movements, he put my silk panties back to rights and tugged my skirt down around my hips, somehow managing to do so even though I was sitting on the bed.

He stepped away, his expression tortured as he looked at me. "I'm going to leave now, and I hope you'll meet me for dinner next week."

I didn't even know how to feel about the crushing sense of disappointment that shafted through me—disappointment that he had enough control to leave, and that he wasn't proposing dinner tomorrow night. Because I didn't want to wait.

"I'll be out of town for the next few days," he continued, promptly answering my unspoken question. "I should be back by Sunday. If you'll say yes, I have a surprise."

I shimmied my hips off the edge of the bed, straightening my skirt and smoothing it over my legs. "What's the surprise?"

Chapter Twenty

RYAN

I glared at the speakerphone on the desk in my hotel suite. "Seriously, Trixie?"

"I'm quite serious, Ryan," Trixie returned in her usual haughty tone. "Even though I only just met Addie the other day, she's practically family. Her aunt was one of my dearest friends. If you hurt Addie, you'll have to answer to me."

Good thing Trixie couldn't see me. Since I was out of town for meetings in Washington, DC, I had conferenced in for the monthly board meeting for the rescue program. Trixie had asked me to call her directly when the session ended. My mouth fell open at her comment. Not because I thought I would hurt Addie, but because I was taken off guard by her protectiveness.

I snapped my mouth shut and gave my head a quick shake. "Trixie, I'm not going to hurt Addie."

"How can you be sure?" she countered swiftly. I could practically feel her sharp gaze pinned on me through the phone line. Trixie was a commanding presence. Age had only reinforced her tendency not to give a shit what anybody thought of her speaking her mind.

I started to reply but paused. It wasn't as if I could guarantee anything. That pause, that moment of hesitation, ended up reinforcing how I felt.

"Look, Trixie, I understand why you might be concerned. I'm not exactly known for taking relationships seriously." Trixie snorted, and I continued. "I like Addie. She's different for me."

I suddenly felt as if I had stumbled onto another planet. Emotionally speaking, that is.

I didn't have much time to ponder, because Trixie replied after a harrumph. "Well, I was right then."

The subtle satisfaction I heard in her tone elicited a chuckle from me. "Please, do tell me what you were right about."

"When Addie told me you helped her after her little incident at your place, and you showed up with her at the fundraiser, something felt different. I'm wondering if I need to be more concerned about your feelings than hers."

A brief sense of panic tightened in my chest. I shook it off and stared at the phone. "Perhaps you do. Obviously, I'm no expert at romance." I got another snort for that comment from Trixie. "I have no intention of hurting Addie. I only hope she actually gives me a chance," I said, completely meaning it.

Trixie was quiet for several beats before finally replying, "I hope so too. Honestly, I don't know her particularly well, but I sensed you two just might be perfect for each other. I've always known you had a heart of gold. Your only lesson—your only example set forth by your parents'—was the cold misery a marriage can be between two people who don't love each other."

———

Trixie's words echoed in my thoughts later as I took the elevator in my hotel downstairs to get a drink at the bar. Graham also happened to be in DC for a few days. We were both here on business. Striding into the bar, my gaze traveled around the room, taking in the plethora of men in suits and women in sharp business attire. My eyes finally found Graham, seated at a small table in the corner by the windows looking out over the city.

I crossed the room quickly, slipping into the chair across from him. "Well, hello there."

Graham glanced up with a wink. "Hi there. Is your conference as boring as mine?"

As I lifted my hand to catch the attention of the waiter nearby, I replied, "For me, it's business meetings. Some are more boring than others."

The waiter stopped by our table, and I ordered a scotch.

"I'll take another," Graham said quickly.

After the waiter left to get our drinks, Graham and I began chatting, covering the usual topics, which were mostly business. As soon as our drinks were delivered, we were interrupted by Elaine Roble, a business acquaintance and a woman I'd taken to a few social events in New York City. Elaine was dressed in what could be considered her uniform, a fitted white blouse that teased her cleavage and a thin, navy pencil skirt.

"I didn't know you were going to be in

town," Elaine said with a warm smile when she stopped beside our table. "Did you two travel here together?"

Graham shook his head. "We didn't travel together, but just happened to be here at the same time. Always good to see you, Elaine," Graham said smoothly.

"I'm here for business meetings," I added when Elaine's gaze shifted to me.

"I don't suppose you two might like company?" Elaine asked, her eyes lingering on me.

I knew that look. It was the look I got from Elaine when she wanted to utilize our friendly-acquaintances-with-benefits relationship. It wasn't something we did often, but it was what it was. I had absolutely *no* interest. Zero wasn't low enough for how uninterested I was.

I smiled tightly and hoped Graham let this slide. "Graham and I are actually discussing some confidential business matters. A pleasure to see you though, Elaine."

I caught the surprised look on Graham's face out of the corner of my eye. Elaine was undeterred. "What about tomorrow night? I'll still be in town if you will."

I kept my smile bland. "Thank you, but I have another business dinner tomorrow night."

I hoped this wasn't going to get any more awkward than necessary and was relieved when another business acquaintance stopped by the table, effectively interrupting our conversation.

Moments later, when it was just Graham and me again, Graham gave me a knowing look. "What's that about?"

I rolled my eyes. "Nothing."

"Oh, it's definitely not nothing. Want to know what I think?"

"I doubt I do, but I'm confident you'll tell me anyway."

Graham chuckled and took a swallow of his scotch. "You like Addie. You *really* like her."

"Why do you think that?" I hedged.

"Because, unlike you, I know what it's like to be in love. Soraya's the best thing that ever happened to me. I'm not claiming you're in love with Addie. It might be too soon for that, but I saw the way you looked at her. For what it's worth, I like Addie. She's good for you."

For a moment, I wanted to shrug Graham's comments off. Yet, he was one of the few friends who knew me well. Graham knew Colin and me when we were growing up together, and he knew the misery of living with my parents because he'd seen it firsthand. I also trusted his judgment, which was not something I could say about many people.

Graham's voice broke into my train of thoughts. "I only have one other thing to say."

"What's that?"

"A woman like Addie doesn't come along often. Don't screw it up."

Graham's words struck at the heart of a fear I'd never experienced before. Because I had no fucking clue how to handle this thing with Addie.

I took a gulp of scotch, needing the fortitude. "I do like her. Since you're you, I'll admit I'm scared to death I'm going to fuck it up. You know what my parents were like."

Graham shrugged. "Yeah, your dad was a fucking asshole, and your mother drank to numb herself to the man he was. Still though, you and Colin took care of each other. You're not the cold, ruthless asshole you let the media think you are. If it helps, it's obvious Addie likes you too." He offered a small smile at that.

For a man whose entire adult life had been shaped to ensure control, the way my heart pounded in my chest and the uncertainty that jolted me wasn't exactly comfortable. I didn't want to be so concerned about how one single person felt about me. And yet, here I was with my tricky heart giving a funny tumble at my friend's comment that Addie liked me too.

I enjoyed my drinks with Graham that evening, and he had enough sense—or rather he knew me well enough—to let the topic of Addie drop after that. As if it hadn't already been sufficiently overwhelming for me.

The following morning, Hazel left me a cryptic message. Hazel rarely left me voice messages. She was insanely organized and usually had my life orchestrated down to the minute. She emailed and texted my daily schedule and any supporting documents I needed for upcoming meetings.

A phone message from her was so rare that I presumed there must be an emergency and called her immediately.

"Good morning, Ryan," Hazel said in her clipped and efficient tone.

"Good morning. You left a phone message asking me to call as soon as I got it. I just got it. Is everything okay?"

"Everything's fine. I had a call from the attorney who handled your brother's estate. She said Colin asked her to contact you regarding some test results that were supposed to be run a few years after your father's death."

I gripped the phone tightly in my hand, leaning my hips against the desk in my hotel suite. I felt briefly unsteady on my feet. "Okaaa-y," I said slowly, hoping my tone didn't belie the tension knotting inside my gut.

"She said you would know what it's about. I'll text you the phone number, okay?"

I imagined Hazel was curious, but she hadn't known me since I was a little boy for nothing. She would wait until I was ready to talk. I wasn't even close to ready now.

"Thank you, Hazel."

"Of course." There was a long pause, and I was about to say goodbye when Hazel spoke again. "If you think whatever this news is might be distracting for you, perhaps you might wait to call," she said gently.

"Always looking out for me, aren't you?"

"Absolutely. I'll see you in the office on Monday. You know where to reach me if anything comes up in the meantime."

"I do. Have a good day, Hazel. Thanks for the call."

"Of course."

The line clicked in my ear, and I slowly lowered my phone after tapping the screen to close it. I felt almost sick. Of all the days to get this phone call. I was already unsettled about Addie after my conversation with Graham last night. Burying my attention in spreadsheets and picking apart a business proposal this morning had helped allay that sense of unease.

Now, a day I both dreaded and anticipated was here. I'd known about this day ever since a conversation I had with my brother six months before his death. I'd purposefully never marked it on my calendar, although I was dimly aware today was that day.

I usually listened to Hazel's advice. She offered it quite rarely. My phone vibrated in my hand. Glancing down, I saw Hazel's promised text message with the name and phone number of the attorney.

Chapter Twenty-One

ADDIE

Crossing my legs, I glanced down at my worn leather cowboy boot. These were my beloved boots, and I'd had them for years. The stitching was starting to break down, and I might have to see if I could find another pair. I didn't want to let them go. The leather was so soft and worn, and they fit my feet and calves like an old friend.

The sound of the door opening in the small examining room drew my attention. Daniel stepped into the room, casting me a quick smile.

"Hi there, Addie. Let me take a look at that hand. I'm going to take it personally if it's not healing perfectly."

I held out my hand with a smiled. "It's

healing well, and all the stitches are dissolved except that little bit sticking out. I was going to yank it out myself, but when I called my mother and mentioned it, she told me I was being ridiculous. So here I am."

Daniel looked down, his eyes skimming over the fresh scars quickly. "You're right. It looks great. It's been a few weeks, so I'm glad to see the stitches are dissolved. I'll yank that last bit out."

He fetched a pair of tweezers and took care of it. "It didn't even hurt," I commented, relieved for that.

Daniel set the tweezers down on a tray, spinning in the chair he'd sat down on to fetch some disinfectant and a cotton ball. After he dabbed over the small pink area of skin, he tossed the cotton ball in one of those biohazard containers and turned back to face me. "You should be good as new. This scar won't stay pink for long."

"Thank you so much," I said. "My insurance deductible thanks you for coming over at Ryan's call to take care of my hand that night too. I'm wondering how soon I can look into getting this tattoo repaired." I gestured to the area where the vine had been broken by one of the scars.

Daniel glanced down at the scar and back

to me. "It's fully healed, and it's a narrow break, but I'd give it time for the pinkness to fade."

"Got it. Thank you again."

Daniel chuckled. "I was happy to do it. How is your dog? I can't recall his name."

"Barnable is fine. He's adjusted to New York City now, but more importantly, the gate in the back of that courtyard is locked now."

"Good to know. And how are you adjusting to New York City? Quite the change from New Orleans, I would imagine."

"Oh, definitely. New Orleans is a different city, but then so many things are the same. People are people everywhere. Although, people do talk a lot faster here."

Daniel threw his head back with a laugh at that. "That they do. It was nice to see you out with Ryan the other night. He's a good man."

We'd briefly encountered Daniel at the charity fundraiser the week prior. I felt like Daniel was trying to convey more than that to me, but I certainly didn't know him well enough to pry. I had just about a million questions for him though.

"Ryan's a personal friend of yours, then?"

"Most definitely. I knew him and his

brother growing up. We went to school together. Ryan is a private man."

I interjected. "I can tell."

Daniel flashed me another grin. "That
said, I'll add he's far more than the man you
read about."

I looked up into his eyes, wondering if I
could be nosy. Honestly, I was an inquisitive
person, but I tried to manage it. Since he had
opened the door for questions, I walked right
through.

"I've gathered as much. What I can't
figure out is why he might want more than
one date with me."

Daniel's smile was wide when he chuckled
softly. "I can't speak for Ryan, but I can take
a guess."

"Please do."

"He likes you, and I think you're good for
him."

"I can only guess I'm nothing like the
women he usually dates. I'm not a model, I
don't dress boring, and I talk back."

"Exactly," Daniel said.

Just then, there was a light knock on the
door.

"Yes?" Daniel called over his shoulder,
casting me an apologetic smile. "I presume
my next appointment is already here."

"No need to apologize. Thank you again for taking care of my hand," I said, lifting it up and wiggling it back and forth.

"My pleasure. Do me a favor," he added as I stood from my chair.

"What?"

"Sometimes Ryan can be an asshole. Ignore him when he does that. Don't let it get in your way."

———

I was far too aware of the fact Ryan had been scheduled to return from his business trip out of town last night. It wasn't as if he had made me promises, but there was a corner of my heart that was disappointed he hadn't called or texted last night.

Yet, I had plenty to do. Today, I'd decided I was going to visit Rockefeller Center and go ice-skating. Growing up in the warm, balmy embrace of New Orleans, there were no chances to ice skate outside. Although my mother had humored me and taken me to lessons at a local skating rink.

I adjusted my scarf around my neck and walked down the street, enjoying the hustle and bustle surrounding me. The energy of New York was so different from what I was accustomed to. It was loud and bustling with sharp noises and an almost constant sense that something was happening nearby, whether you were a part of it or not.

I stopped to get a warm pretzel with mustard, savoring the soft bread and the tang of the mustard as I took a bite. I finally found my way to Rockefeller Center. After I got my ticket, I pulled my ice skates out of my bag and leaned over to put them on one of the benches outside the rink.

When I was a little girl, I'd seen a movie with a romantic scene in this very ice-skating rink. Coming here was a childhood dream come true. Although I'd only visited Eleanor once, I remembered her and my mother walking me down here so I could see the rink. At that time, I hadn't even skated before, so I wasn't allowed out on the ice.

No one could stop me today. After stuffing my cowboy boots away in my backpack, I stepped through the gate and onto the ice. I started slow, making sure to get my footing and balance.

I spun in slow circles amongst the other skaters who were also enjoying this clear winter day. I savored the feel of the icy air as I picked up speed. The cold was bracing and made me feel so alive. I glided over the ice, enjoying every second of it. The air was biting as the sun disappeared behind the clouds. I didn't stop until a light snow began to fall from the sky.

The crowd began to thin out, and I spun in a circle in the center of the rink before I decided it was time to go home. Skating to the edge, I heard my name and glanced around to see Ryan with his elbows braced on the railing.

My heart set off at a thrumming beat, and joy spun through me like glitter.

I skated over to where Ryan was waiting, resting my hands on the railing between his when I almost lost my balance as I came to a stop a little too quickly.

"Hey," I said, feeling my lips tug into a smile.

I didn't know how Ryan pulled it off, but every single time I saw him, the look in his eyes had butterflies massing in my belly and sparks scattering through my body.

He wore his typical suit with a light wool jacket over it. He was such a quintessential wealthy New York businessman. Yet, the glint in his eye was intense, and he looked more somber than usual. I thought I saw a hint of sadness flickering in his gaze, but then

I couldn't argue to know him all that well. Not yet.

"How did you find me?" I asked.

"I was walking by to get an evening cup of coffee and saw you."

There were people everywhere. It was New York City, in Rockefeller Center. I imagined the city would be busy even in the worst weather. A little bit of snow falling from the sky like glitter wasn't going to sway the crowds milling about the various food stands and passing by on the way to wherever they happened to be going in the wild pulse of this city.

Despite the crowds surrounding us, I felt as if we were all alone as his gaze held mine. "Oh. Where's your coffee?" I noticed he didn't have anything in his hands.

"I thought I'd wait for you. I was hoping I could persuade you to have dinner with me."

"Yes!"

The moment that single, joyful word jumped out of my mouth, I wanted to snatch it back. I needed to be a little bit more, well, calm about all this. I needed to play it cool. My intellectual brain and my smartly guarded heart were in agreement on this. But there was that little part of me that was ever hopeful and wishful against all of my better judgment. And apparently, Ryan's influence over that small part of me appeared to have taken hold in this moment.

Ryan shifted, sliding his hands inward on the railing until they curled over mine. "You're freezing, Addie," he said, concern forming a crease between his brows.

"I thought I came prepared, but I forgot my gloves. I'm not used to even thinking about gloves," I said with a sheepish shrug.

"Come on, let's get you out of those skates and get you somewhere warm."

I stood there, smiling at him like a fool. Time felt suspended for several beats of my heart until Ryan leaned forward and closed the distance between us. When his lips met mine, it was an electric shock to my system, rippling outward through my body. His lips were warm, and I was cold. In another second, I shifted closer to the railing and rose to meet him as his tongue swept in to glide sensually against mine.

Far too soon, he drew back, murmuring against my lips, "You are too much."

When he lifted his head, I asked, "Too much what?"

Ryan stared at me while blood rushed in my ears and I felt my arousal slick between my thighs. "Too much everything."

I shivered again.

"Your hair is getting wet from the snow, Addie. Come on."

He released one of my hands and turned to begin walking. I glided along on the other side of the railing with our fingers laced together. He didn't let go of my hand until I got to the gate. I needed both of mine to step out and unlace my ice skates. People moved around us, and the hum of conversation carried on. Ryan was the only thing my awareness centered on.

"Where are your shoes?" he asked as I stepped out of one boot.

Standing on one leg, I wobbled slightly, and he caught my elbow to steady me. "In my backpack," I muttered.

"Mind if I get them out for you?"

"Please do."

A few minutes later, I had my cowboy boots on, and Ryan carefully returned my ice skates into the case I'd stuffed in my backpack.

"Ready?"

At his question, I looked up. My heartbeat skidded and jumpstarted as I stared into his deep blue eyes with the snow falling down around us.

"Yes."

Ryan's hand caught mine, his grip warm and firm. "How come you're not cold?" I teased as we began walking down the street.

He lifted a shoulder in an easy shrug. "It's not too bad out. I'm more used to the cold than I'd guess you are."

"Where are we going?"

He stopped on the sidewalk, glancing up toward the snow, which had begun to fall a bit more heavily. Leveling his eyes with mine again, he asked, "How about we order the best Thai takeout in the city and go back to my place?"

"Can we stop and get Barnable on the way? He could use the walk."

"Absolutely. I'd love to have dinner with you and Barnable."

Chapter Twenty-Two

ADDIE

After we stopped to fetch Barnable, and I fed him dinner, we walked the two blocks from my place to Ryan's, picking up the promised Thai takeout on the way. When we stepped into Ryan's pristine entryway, Barnable tugged on his leash. Glancing up to Ryan, I asked, "Is it okay if I let him loose?"

Ryan looked down at Barnable before leaning over to scratch between his ears. Straightening, he replied, "Of course. I wouldn't have said you could bring him over if he couldn't be loose. This time, he's not bleeding."

His eyes glinted with mirth, and I rolled mine in return. Leaning down, I unclipped Barnable's leash and gave him a pat on his round bottom. "Off you go. You can inspect the place."

"Feel free to hang up your jacket." Ryan gestured to the coat rack just beyond a table by the door. He shrugged out of his own jacket as he spoke, setting the bag of takeout food on the table as he did.

I followed suit and hung my jacket and toed off my boots, which were covered in snow. We'd almost decided to go to my place but stuck with this plan since my home wasn't fully furnished yet. Although I'd made some progress in the house, the older furniture wasn't particularly comfortable.

Barnable's claws tapped on the hardwood flooring as he trotted off to explore. The tile floor was cool on my feet through my stockings.

Turning, I looked up at Ryan. We stared at each other for a beat before he reached for my hand. "Come on," he said gruffly. "I'll show you the sitting room."

With my heartbeat galloping along at a fast clip, I followed him down the hallway. Pausing outside the archway that led into the kitchen, Ryan released my hand.

"Hang on, just dropping this off." He stepped away to deposit the take-out bag on a low counter right inside the kitchen.

In another second, he was back at my side, and once again, his hand curled around mine. I didn't want to think too hard about how good it felt to have his warm, strong grip engulfing my hand. For crying out loud, he was just holding my hand.

It felt so good and was somehow reassuring. All the while, my body was tossed asunder with my pulse running wild, my breath coming in shallow pants, and heat spinning in pinwheels through my body.

"Right here," he said as he led me through another archway into a room. The lights came on as we stepped in, immediately dimming when Ryan reached to the side and adjusted the switch on the wall.

My gaze scanned the room. There was a large sectional couch in a soft gray in the center of the room. Unlike the hallway and kitchen, this room had carpeting, and my footfalls were silent as I followed him over. He pressed a button on the wall, and flames came to life in the dark fireplace, instantly casting a warm glow through the room.

A large flat-screen TV was mounted on the wall above the fireplace. I looked up at Ryan. "This is cozy."

The light from the flames flickering beside us cast his face half in shadow. I took him in—the clean, strong lines of his face with his sculpted cheekbones, his straight nose, and his square jaw. That look I'd seen in his eyes when he leaned over the railing to kiss me was back.

There was an intensity I didn't quite know how to read contained there. His gaze searched my face, and I wanted to ask what he was thinking. Thought fled my mind when he stepped closer and lifted his hand, tracing a fingertip lightly over one of my brows. His touch trailed down my cheek before his thumb traced my bottom lip.

Everywhere he touched felt like fire shimmering over the surface of my skin.

"How was your trip?" I heard myself asking, marveling that in a corner of my mind I could even think to ask a single question.

His shoulders lifted in a slight shrug as he stepped a little closer. We weren't touching, but it felt as if the space between us, no more than an inch, was electrified.

"It was fine. I missed you."

I was caught in his hypnotizing gaze. His words surprised me. Ryan didn't strike me as a man to share his feelings easily, nor did he seem like the kind of man who would miss anyone. Certainly not me.

My heart gave a resounding thump, its

beat echoing through my entire body. Almost as if in punctuation to his last three words.

I'd missed him, but I wasn't quite ready to admit that. This was all too surprising, all too unexpected.

I didn't know who moved first, but suddenly I was pressed against him and stretching up. I absolutely *had* to kiss him. It couldn't wait another second.

The first brush of my lips against his was a subtle, almost glancing touch. Ryan's breath drew in sharply, hissing through his teeth as he lifted his head as if shocked.

On the heels of that, he murmured, "Addie."

It was just one word, my name, but he said it with such emotion and force, I felt it reverberating through every corner of my heart. In a flash, his lips were on mine again, and I lost sense of everything else. We tumbled into that kiss as if we were diving into the depths of the ocean together, clinging to each other to keep from drowning in the mad rush of desire.

Ryan's strong arms wrapped around me to mold me against him, while his tongue delved in deeply to tease against mine. He dropped little kisses at the corners of my mouth with his teeth catching my bottom lip as he drew back. The feel of the hard, hot length of his cock pressing against my lower belly sent a gush of arousal between my thighs. Goosebumps chased over my skin when he dusted kisses on the side of my neck, and blood rushed through my ears with every beat of my heart as sensation caught me in its wake and pulled me under.

I distantly heard myself gasping Ryan's name as his lips made their way in a fiery trail down the side of my neck. He lifted his head, his eyes meeting mine. The look there stole my breath, and my knees went weak as my belly spun wildly in flips.

The effect this man had on me was unlike anything I'd ever experienced before. I would've done just about anything he said in the moment. Fortunately for me, it seemed all he wanted was me.

He lifted a hand from where it had been wrapped around my waist to cup my cheek as he stared into my eyes. "I want you."

His words were a drum beat, and my heart thudded in reply.

"I'll stop if you want, but if that's the case, we should stop now."

I could feel his body almost vibrating with restraint. His touch was light on my cheek, and I knew he meant every word he said. He would stop, and this would go no further. I opened my mouth to reply when he spoke again. "To clarify, I'll stop whenever you want. It's just..." His eyes fell closed, and he took a breath before opening them again. "I need you."

"I don't want to stop," I said, speaking the plain truth. I wanted Ryan with a raw, burning need I no longer wanted to fight. No matter what, I wanted to see this through because if I didn't, I would always wonder what I'd missed.

His eyes closed yet again, and I didn't hear what he said before his lips crashed to mine. We tumbled back into the madness, the rushing current sweeping us right back to where we'd been.

Ryan's kisses were beyond dangerous to my sanity. He swept away any defenses as he devoured my mouth. I didn't even realize he'd moved us until the backs of my knees bumped against the edge of the couch, and I let out a surprised gasp.

Ryan murmured something against my skin, his lips teasing along an insanely sensitive spot on the side of my neck just below my ear. Dear God. I hadn't known I could get so needy just from the motion of his lips right there.

He chuckled when I clutched at his shoulders and murmured, "For God's sake, you're driving me crazy."

He lifted his head, his eyes teasing and dark and filled with so much naughtiness I wanted to twine myself around him like a vine and never let go.

"That's the point," he said with enough deliberateness that I felt like he had a bit too much control in the situation. I never did like a man having the upper hand.

I let my fingers trail across his chest and bit my bottom lip. "You might be driving me crazy, but I can return the favor." I dragged my hand across his belly and cupped my palm over the hard ridge of his arousal. Ryan let out a low growl as I boldly squeezed. "You know, I never knew a man could wear a suit this well," I murmured, appreciating how well his slacks defined his cock. Not that I would have expected anything less, but Ryan was clearly well endowed.

I deftly undid his belt and fly in a hot second, discovering that he wore fitted boxer briefs. As I slipped my hand over his blatant arousal, he let out another hissed breath through his teeth.

"Enough," he ordered.

I giggled because it was fun to rile Ryan

up. He was so suave, so alpha, so controlled that there was something particularly decadent about snatching his precious control out of his hands.

He spun around, lifting me against him as he sat down on the couch with me a bundle in his lap. "Oh, this is perfect!" I exclaimed.

My knees fell to either side of his hips as I straddled him, and my skirt rode up around my hips. I was wearing a pair of wool tights underneath, which did little to disguise the heat of his arousal when I pressed down over it. Pleasure pierced through me in a jolt. I was slick with arousal, and my clit was swollen. Nothing more than the subtle pressure of him against me nearly pushed me over the edge.

That little burst of pleasure gave Ryan a moment to regain control. He tugged at the buttons of my blouse until it fell open. His lips pressed like a hot brand in the valley between my breasts. He wasted no time flicking the clasp of my bra open, roughly cupping one breast and leaning forward to catch my nipple with his teeth. The warm suction had me spearing my fingers in his hair and crying out as I arched into him.

Frantic to feel more of him, I yanked at the buttons on his shirt, not caring that one broke loose and disappeared into the cushions of the couch. Ryan's chest was simply glorious, lightly dusted with dark hair and all hard muscles. His skin was warm to the touch as I mapped the muscled planes with my palms.

He lifted his head, pinning me with his intense gaze as he lightly pinched one of my nipples. I squirmed on his lap.

"You have too many clothes on," I gasped when he flexed his hips slightly as I rocked mine into him.

"So do you," he murmured.

Because he was strong, and apparently also very efficient, Ryan lifted me and yanked my skirt and wool stockings down in one quick motion. "Fuck, Addie. You're killing me."

"That's not my plan," I managed to tease.

His eyes swept up and down my body, his look downright dirty. Reaching out, he hooked his finger over the elastic edge of my panties and tugged me between his knees. When he leaned forward and dropped hot kisses over my belly, heat radiated through me at every point where his lips met my flushed skin.

He lifted his head, his eyes almost level with mine with me standing and him seated.

"I didn't expect you to have a thing for black lace." His voice was low and taut and sent a shiver through my entire body.

I was quivering with need and shifted my thighs to ease the ache building there. "I have a thing for lace," I finally choked out.

Ryan's fingers teased over my belly before dipping down between my thighs to cup my mound. "I didn't know I did. Until you."

I meant to say something, I swear I did, but then he shoved my black lace and silk panties out of the way and stroked his fingers through my folds. I let out a little moan just before he sank two fingers in my channel. I almost came right then. I clung to my control—what little I had—because I didn't want to climax, not yet. I wanted the full experience with Ryan buried inside of me.

"Don't," I gasped as my hips rocked into the next stroke of his fingers.

He stilled immediately. "Okay."

I was confused for a moment before I realized he thought I was trying to stop the entire encounter. "I don't mean we're stopping," I clarified as I reached to free his cock from his boxer briefs. "It's just I don't want to come until you're inside of me."

Ryan's breath drew in sharply. For a long

moment, all I could hear was the sound of my heartbeat thundering through my body.

Then, he was reaching to yank out his wallet, a condom packet falling on the couch as he did. In a matter of seconds, he'd rolled it on and was drawing me back toward him. I could've tried to argue the point I was in control, but I *so* absolutely wasn't.

I wanted Ryan, so fiercely, I couldn't see or think beyond it. All I knew was I needed to be fused with him and to find the sweet release I craved.

With our shirts torn open and both of us still half dressed, this was a rushed, messy encounter, and I didn't even care. His hands gripped my hips lightly, stopping my motion as I began to move.

"What?" That single word question came out demanding. Desire was driving me, and I needed to seek relief.

"I didn't want to rush this, but you're not giving me much choice," he murmured.

"We can take our time next time," I gasped, and I felt the press of his cockhead teasing at my entrance.

"Is that a promise?"

Although his words held a teasing hint, I sensed he was dead serious.

"Absolutely."

I meant it too. Because this might be crazy, but I knew I was going to need more than just this to burn Ryan Blake out of my system.

With his eyes hot on mine, Ryan eased his grip. I slowly lowered down, letting out a satisfied hum as he filled and stretched me.

I couldn't look away. With him watching me, this moment of joining was incredibly intense. The look in his eyes was so intimate I almost couldn't bear it.

Chapter Twenty-Three

RYAN

Addie's wide, dark eyes held me ensnared. I didn't want to look away, and I couldn't even if I'd tried. With every echoing beat of my heart, I felt more connected to her in this moment than I'd ever felt to anyone.

I wanted to trick myself into thinking it was merely the hottest sex I'd ever had—and it most definitely was—but it was so much more. When she sank down over me, sheathing me in her slick, clenching core, our physical fusion sent sensation upon sensation careening through me.

She let out this little breathy hum, and it was like a whip lashing me, driving me to sink deeper and deeper into her even though I was already buried to the hilt. I meant what I said—that I hadn't wanted to rush this, but it was a force well beyond my control.

I'd always been inclined to set the tone and pace of any sexual encounter and usually had no trouble keeping my grip firmly on the reins of control. Yet, with Addie, everything was scrambled, and I felt as if I were skidding out of control.

I had no idea what a turn on it would be to experience her sassy attempt to take control. Fuck. It was downright intoxicating and only strengthened my resolve to try to retain what little control I had.

Addie rose up slightly, almost pushing me over the edge. I gripped her hips more tightly, savoring the generous give of her flesh under my fingers. The downside to never letting myself get involved was I tended to end up in these acquaintance-with-benefits relationships with high society types who wouldn't dare let any curves develop. Little did they know, I loved a woman with curves. Addie had them in spades. Her lush breasts bounced slightly as she shifted. The feel of her nipples, puckered tight and brushing against my chest was enough to drive me mad.

"Easy," I murmured when she wiggled impatiently.

She let out a gasp before leaning forward to press a hot kiss along my jawline and nip my neck before lifting her head. I could see the frustration flashing in her eyes, and I couldn't help but let out a low chuckle.

"Impatient?"

"I should think that's obvious," she murmured when she wiggled again.

This time, I let go, letting my head fall back when she rose up and sank down, sheathing me inside of her again as her slick channel rippled around my cock.

I watched while she set a steady rhythm, biting her lip, a little whimper escaping as I flexed just enough to create friction right where her clit rubbed against me. Our angle was such that there wasn't much for me to do. Every motion was a slow pull and glide as she sank down over me again and again and again.

She gasped my name when I grabbed her waist, bringing her down rapidly while I flexed into the roll of her hips. I'd never cared, not one bit if a woman cried my name in passion. Yet, when Addie did, I fucking loved it.

My release was threatening, as my balls tightened and electricity bundled at the base of my spine. As she rose up, I reached between us, pressing my thumb right where we were joined. When she came down, she cried out, her entire body going taut, and her pussy clenching hard around my length.

When Addie shuddered and cried my name once more, I finally let go, my own release slamming through me so hard, and abruptly, it was a damn good thing I was already sitting down. By the time my consciousness flickered through the tumult of sensation, Addie was curled against my chest with her chin tucked into the side of my neck. The feel of her breath gusting softly across my skin was the first thing I noticed when conscious thought broke through the haze of desire.

I glanced down. Her cheeks were flushed. My eyes traveled further down to where one of her breasts was pressed against my chest with her skin dewy in the flickering light from the fireplace. With her blouse open, her bra hanging to the sides, and her skirt hitched around her waist, she looked like a complete mess. So did I.

I certainly wasn't prone to being so enthralled by a woman that I fucked in a rush on the couch with my clothes barely off.

But then, this was Addie. There were no

rules when it came to her. I threw them all away.

Case in point: when I heard the sound of Barnable's claws clicking down the hallway and going quiet as he padded into this room with the carpet muffling the sound, that should've been my cue to gracefully and dispassionately untangle us. Instead, I let my fingers sift through her silky hair and said, "I think we have company."

Addie giggled and lifted her head, turning to glance over her shoulder. Looking up, I saw that Barnable appeared more curious about the fire than us as he waddled over to stare into the flickering flames.

Addie looked back at me, and my heart gave a rib cracking kick. She bit her lip as her eyes searched my face. "Is this when I should graciously get dressed and leave?"

"Absolutely not. We still have dinner. You're not going anywhere tonight."

———

The following morning, my awareness came in fragments as I came awake. The soft curve of Addie's bottom pressed against my arousal. My hand at rest on her belly. The easy rhythm of her breath, quiet and steady as she slept. The scent of her winding around me as I breathed her in where my head was resting on the pillow behind hers.

I thought I couldn't have experienced a deeper sense of intimacy than our rushed, intense, and explosive encounter last night. Yet, waking up beside her with winter sunlight spilling through the windows and angling across the bed held a more profound sense of intimacy. It had an almost mundane quality to it. Because what could be more simple, and necessary than sleep? The vulnerability it took to actually fall asleep with someone else was something I'd never contemplated.

Although my arousal was rather insistent, I didn't want to act on it. Maybe another time after I'd had more than one night tangled up with Addie sound asleep at my side. But this morning, I didn't want to ruin the moment, didn't want to let my lust, ever-present when I was near her, to overtake this moment.

Because I couldn't help it, I let my palm lazily caress over the sweet curve of her hip and back up her side. I traced my fingertips along her collarbone before I brushed her hair away from her face and pressed a kiss on her cheek. I was startled out of my hazy awareness when I felt motion at my feet on the bed.

Lifting my head, I was greeted by the site of Barnable's cheerful face with his chubby little paws resting on the foot of my bed as he peered over the edge of the mattress. My body shook lightly with my chuckle, and Addie murmured something.

"Yes?" I asked.

She rolled over in my arms, promptly stealing my breath. Fuck me. Addie was gorgeous on her own, this bright spot in my life I'd never expected. Yet, Addie unguarded in the morning was shockingly beautiful.

Her dark hair was tousled against the white pillows, and her cheeks were slightly flushed from sleep with the crinkle of the pillowcase imprinted on one cheek. She gave me a lazy smile, and my heart responded with several deep thumps.

"Is that Barnable?"

I tore my eyes from hers to look back at him. Although I couldn't see his tail, I presumed he was wagging it because the mattress was vibrating slightly from his excitement. His face disappeared from view with his claws clicking on the floor as he rounded to the side of the bed where Addie was resting. His head popped up immediately beside her.

"Yes, as you can see," I replied, smiling at her.

She reached over, scratching her fingers behind one of his ears. "Fortunately, he can't quite jump on the bed."

"Is that fortunate?" I countered.

Addie shrugged as she rolled her head back to look at me. "Probably. As it is, I spoil him rotten. If he could get on the bed, I wouldn't be able to keep him off, and then he'd think he owned it."

I chuckled, giving in to the temptation to brush my lips over hers. It felt as if a jolt of electricity passed between us. I forced myself to draw back, scrambling to get some control.

Barnable gave me an assist when he let out a soft woof. I rolled away from Addie, mentally shocked at the sharp edge of reluctance I felt. When my feet hit the cool hardwood flooring, I took a deep breath, willing the need pulsing through my body to dissipate. Barnable proved to be good at throwing cold water on that by scurrying around the bed and licking my feet.

I didn't even let myself turn to look at Addie again because her tousled, sleepy temptation would be too much. After I tugged on a pair of sweatpants and a T-shirt, I finally glanced her way to see that she had tugged on the T-shirt and spare sweatpants I'd lent her last night after our encounter. They were definitely too big for her, but she rolled up the sweatpants and tied the T-shirt in a knot at her waist. I never thought I'd give a damn about seeing a woman wearing my clothes, but something about Addie in them sent a jolt of possessiveness through me.

"Do you mind if I wear these for my walk home?" she asked when she looked up.

Wordlessly, I shook my head, ignoring the pounding of my heart and the urge to stride around my bed and yank her back into it.

"Coffee?" I asked when I thought I had myself under control.

"I'll never say no to coffee," she teased. "After that, I need to get going because Barnable needs breakfast." She paused, cocking her head to the side. "What was the surprise?"

For a moment, I didn't know what she was talking about, but then Barnable licked my foot and jogged my memory. "Oh, I want to take you to the rescue program. I thought maybe we could walk some of the dogs."

Addie's smile was like a ray of sun beaming just on me. "I'd love that." Her tone was soft and wondering, and my heart thudded in response.

Not much later, the sound of the front door clicking shut behind Addie when she departed with Barnable at her side echoed in the entryway. I heard my phone vibrating on the kitchen counter as I strode back down the hallway. Lifting it, I saw Hazel's fifth text, this one, *Are you OK? I'm getting worried. You're never late to the office.*

————

Hazel stood on the opposite side of my desk, her fingertips resting lightly on the surface. "Glad to see that you're perfectly okay. Mind filling me in on why you were late? I try not to pry in your personal life," she said this pointedly. "But I get worried. You have never actually been late to work."

"I do apologize, Hazel."

Hazel had been on the phone when I arrived, so I quickly got settled in my office and started plowing through the emails that never seemed to end.

"Is everything okay?" she pressed.

"It's fine, as you can see," I said with a

shrug as I tapped save on my computer keyboard.

"I see that you're fine, but you do seem a little... Well, I don't know how else to put it, but you seem off."

"I went out with Addie last night," I finally said.

While Hazel rarely commented, she did tell me when she liked people, and she'd loved Addie when she met her.

Hazel's lips quirked in a smile. "Oh really? Is that why you're late?"

"Yes. I was only an hour late. I usually get to the office at seven, so arriving at eight isn't exactly an emergency," I said drily.

"For you, it is. I hope you take Addie out to dinner again."

"You do?" I didn't even care that I was taking Hazel's bait.

"Yes, but don't you dare hurt Addie. I like her."

I chuckled. "I don't intend to. I like Addie too."

Hazel flashed a smile and turned to leave my office when the phone rang on her desk. I surprised myself with my next comment.

"I called the attorney. He wasn't my father."

Hazel stood completely still for a moment before turning around slowly, her eyes searching my face.

"It's a relief," I added. "You don't need to worry about me. But what I didn't realize was that he also wasn't Colin's father." Hazel didn't look surprised. "Did you expect that? Because I didn't."

I watched as Hazel closed her eyes, her shoulders rising and falling with a deep breath before she opened them again. "I'm not shocked. Your parents were miserable. Your father—well, I suppose he wasn't your father—was a cold, distant, and emotionally abusive man to your mother. She initially dealt with it by seeking relief in an affair with a man who I suspect is the father of you and Colin. But when your father found out about her affair, he threatened all kinds of things. The only thing he wanted was money. Your mother stayed in the marriage to give him that and protect everything else. I'm sorry she didn't have the strength to cut her losses. Keeping the company under her control meant staying married. That's what she did because she didn't want your father to get it all. She wanted something for you boys, and that company was her father's to begin with."

"I know," I said slowly. "The DNA test said that Colin and I are a ninety-nine percent match. Do you happen to know who that man is, or was?"

Hazel nodded.

"Did he know?" was my next question

Hazel nodded and swallowed, the sound audible in the room. "I think so. Your mother made him stay away, and so he did. Your father threatened to ruin him. He passed away the same year your mother died."

I sat there and absorbed this information. The shockwave of learning my father wasn't my father had been an immense relief. But I didn't know what to think of my mother's role in not letting me know my true father.

Chapter Twenty-Four

ADDIE

I watched as Barnable chased the tennis ball I'd just thrown. He came bounding back, his ears bouncing up and down as he stopped in front of me and dropped the ball at my feet.

"One more," I said as I lifted the ball and tossed it again. When he reliably returned, I got a disappointed look after I tucked the tennis ball into my jacket pocket and clipped his leash on.

"Sorry, but I need to drop you off and get to the grocery store," I explained as we walked out of the park and onto the sidewalk.

The snow had melted, not that there'd been much to begin with, and I looked around as we walked down the sidewalk back toward Aunt Eleanor's place. I wondered if I would ever begin considering it my own. Although it technically was, it was hard for me to think of it that way.

Horns honked and traffic passed by as people hurried down the sidewalk. Since my job allowed me to work from home, I didn't have to rush to get on the subway every morning. I contemplated doing so just for the experience of it. As I was looking around, I heard my name.

Turning, I saw Soraya approaching. She was also walking a small white dog. Soraya smiled when she stopped in front of me. "Is your dog friendly?" she asked.

"Oh yes," I assured her. "Ridiculously so." Barnable was already proving my point as he wagged his short tail so hard, his entire body vibrated while he touched noses with her little dog.

Soraya gestured down to her dog. "Blackie is too. This is actually Graham's dog, but he shares him with me now," she offered with a grin.

I leaned down and held out my gloved hand. After Blackie sniffed it, I stroked down his back while Soraya greeted Barnable. I straightened again. "If you ever need a dog walking partner, just let me know."

"Of course. Where are you headed?"

"Back to my place. It's just a few blocks away. After I drop off Barnable, I'm running a few errands. You?" I asked politely.

I liked Soraya, but she intimidated me a bit. She was stunningly beautiful and had a strong presence. "Back to work for me. I'm running late as it is."

"I don't think I caught what you do for work."

"I'm an assistant for a columnist, Ask Ida."

"Oh! I've seen that column. I love her advice."

Soraya winked. "Well, if you ever have a pressing issue, don't hesitate to write in."

I suddenly recalled a question I'd been meaning to ask anyone familiar with New York City. "You don't happen to have a recommendation for a tattoo artist?"

"I do! Tig's Tattoo and Piercing. It's on Eighth Avenue. Tig is an old friend, and he and his wife own the place. He does great work, and you can totally trust him," Soraya said firmly.

"Oh great. I'll have to check it out. I need to get a tattoo repaired," I explained.

"What happened?"

I lifted my now healed hand. "When I cut

my wrist, it went right through a line on a tattoo. I'd like to get it fixed somehow."

The sound of a phone chiming had me checking my pocket to see if it was mine. Soraya did the same and looked over. "That's me. I'll need to take this. Great to see you, and don't hesitate to call if you'd like to walk together or just hang out."

———

Sexy Suit: *How's your day going?*

When my phone vibrated and I glanced down to see the text from Ryan, a smile curled my lips automatically, and a subtle flush suffused my body. I still hadn't absorbed my night with him. I mentally shied away from it every time I began to contemplate the implications.

The intensity and intimacy of those hours with Ryan were almost shocking. I was feeling anxious about how easily my guard had fallen away. Yet, I couldn't help the little thrill that jolted through me at his text. I replied to him almost instantly.

Me: *My day is fine. Yours?*

Sexy Suit: *I was hoping to see you for dinner tonight, but unfortunately, I have a last-minute meeting.*

Disappointment pierced me. Immediately on the heels of that was a sense of relief. I needed a little time to buttress my defenses, so I didn't get stupid and fall for Ryan. I knew what kind of man he was, and I knew I needed to stay sensible.

My biggest weakness had always been wishing for fairytales in love. That had likely been a reaction to watching my mother long for my emotionally unavailable and entirely absent father.

I tapped out a reply. *No worries. There will be more nights for dinner.*

Just as I tapped send, my phone rang with my mother's name flashing on the screen. I didn't wait to answer.

"Hey, Mama. I'm blowing you a kiss."

My mother laughed softly. "Hello, dear. I'm blowing you a kiss too. How are you?"

I didn't know why, but I instantly sensed worry and sorrow in my mother's voice. We'd always been close, so I didn't hesitate to ask, "What's wrong?"

My mother's sigh filtered through the phone line. "I should've known you could tell I was worried. Before I explain, I just want you to know I love you."

A sense of coldness encircled me, like the

air misting out of the freezer when you opened it. "What is it, Mama?"

"Your father died."

I was relieved I was already sitting down at the kitchen table. For a few seconds, I felt as if I were falling from a great height, tumbling through the air and simply hoping the landing wasn't too brutal.

I took a deep breath and let it out slowly. "Oh wow." Sorrow crashed through me with a wave of regret following on its heels. "What happened?"

"He had a stroke."

"Are you okay?"

My mother was quiet for a moment before answering, "Obviously, I'm sad. But I'll be okay. I said goodbye to your father in pieces over many years."

I knew her words to be true because I'd watched her grieve my father's absence throughout my childhood. He treated her like a cast-off piece of clothing.

Obviously, I wasn't there for the start of my parents' relationship. Rumor had it they had a passionate affair. My father came from a wealthy family, and my mother was young and beautiful. She didn't fit in his world. Although he married her due to pressure from his family and hers when she became pregnant with me, the marriage was only on paper. My father's presence in my life was periodic, and that was being generous. For so long, I wanted him to be there for me, but I eventually accepted he never would be.

Because my mother came from a deeply loving and involved family, I was never short on love, or a sense of belonging. Yet, I still longed for a father. He was the reason I was so cautious about falling for anyone.

As I sat there on the phone with my mother, listening to her worry about me while I worried about her, it occurred to me that I was as much a misfit in Ryan's world as my mother had been in my father's. I didn't know what to think of that.

"When will the funeral be?" I heard myself asking.

"Next week. You don't have to come."

"Of course I'll be there, Mama. I can honor him in death no matter what the state of our relationship was in life. I'll let you know my flight arrangements once they're in place."

"What will you do about Barnable?"

"I'll find someone to take care of him," I replied quickly, realizing I'd need to think fast on that. The first person who came to mind was Ryan.

Chapter Twenty-Five

RYAN

The sound of Barnable's claws clicking on the tile tugged my lips into a smile. He rounded the corner of the large island in the center of my kitchen with one of his ears perking forward when he saw me sitting at the small nook in the corner of the kitchen. I sipped my coffee and patted the side of my leg.

As soon as he reached my side, I scratched behind his ears. "How ya doing, buddy?" I asked conversationally.

Barnable rubbed his head against my calf and made a snuffling sound. "See, you broke in, and now you get to stay here for a few nights."

Barnable looked up at me before meandering over to lap water from the water bowl

I'd set in the corner. When Addie called a few days ago, asking if I minded taking care of him so she could go to her father's funeral, I hadn't hesitated to say yes.

If that didn't put into context the effect she had on me, I didn't know what did. Oh sure, I loved dogs. But I didn't usually volunteer to dog sit, nor did I have any friends who would even think to ask me. I managed my love of dogs by being on the board of the shelter and donating heavily. I preferred to keep those details private.

I tapped my cell phone screen open and called Hazel. She answered on the second ring. "Good morning, Ryan. Are you calling to let me know you're going to be late?"

There wasn't the slightest hint of teasing in her tone, but I knew Hazel well, and I knew she was smiling on the other end of the line. I chuckled. "Actually, no. I was calling to let you know I'm bringing a dog into the office for the day."

There was a long beat of silence after that. "Well, this is the second time you've surprised me in the last few weeks. Actually, make that the third."

"What's the first?" I was genuinely curious. I knew being late had been a surprise.

"When you asked for my help with Addie

and the attorney. That reminds me, our attorney asked me if he should bill us, or her. Do let me know what to tell him."

"Tell him to bill us."

"That's what I figured, but I thought I should check," Hazel replied smoothly. "Now, is there anything you need for your canine companion today? And where did you get a dog?"

Hazel happened to know I loved dogs, but I was about to surprise her again. "I didn't get a dog. I'm taking care of Addie's dog. She needed to go out of town for a few days."

Once again, because I knew Hazel well, I could practically see one of her eyebrows arching up on the other end of the phone line. "Shall I get a water bowl?" she asked politely.

"Good idea. Thank you for taking care of that."

Not much later, I glanced from Barnable to the bright blue knitted sweater Addie had given me when she dropped him off yesterday. "What do you think?" I asked Barnable as I leaned down and held the sweater up for his inspection.

Barnable sniffed at it and stepped back with a suspicious look. When I placed the sweater on his back, he gave a hard shake. Out of loyalty to Addie, I tried again, even though I thought a dog sweater was ridiculous.

Barnable shook again. "All right, we won't do the sweater, but you have to explain if Addie finds out."

I convinced myself that Barnable's tail wag indicated he agreed with me. Off we went to my office.

I had to admit I enjoyed Barnable's company. He was so curious as he looked around cheerfully on the walk to the office. I could've called my driver, but I generally preferred the walk when the weather was good. It was chilly this morning, but Barnable didn't seem to mind it.

I arrived to discover that Hazel—efficient as always—had gotten a water bowl, dog treats, and a dog bed. Barnable was apparently going to be spoiled everywhere he went.

Late that afternoon, I stepped out of my office after a meeting to find Barnable happily curled up on his new bed beside Hazel's desk. She glanced over with a smile. "I knew Addie was good for you," she announced.

"I'm not even going to argue with you on that point, Hazel."

Hazel's hands stilled on her keyboard, and she swiveled in her chair to face me. "It took an effort for my mouth not to fall open," she said solemnly as she eyed me.

I leaned over to scratch behind Barnable's ears. "I don't mind admitting it. I like Addie."

When I straightened, Hazel's gaze searched my face carefully as a slow smile stretched across hers. "Good. It's about time you stopped treating dating like a business."

I rested my hip against the edge of her desk. "Addie's different."

"You've dated plenty of accomplished, beautiful women."

"Addie is quite beautiful, but that's not why it's hard to resist her."

I couldn't believe I was being this open. Yet, somehow learning that the man who'd raised me and who was so cold and harsh—and frankly the opposite of loving—wasn't my father had been a considerable relief. I'd always feared I might become him, and therefore found it easier not to look for more in the realm of relationships.

Hazel studied me for another beat before nodding slowly. "I completely agree with you."

"Now that's rare," I teased.

"Only when it comes to personal matters.

I've always agreed with you when it came to business," she said tartly. Her gaze sobered. "How are you doing with the news?"

"It's a relief," I replied, knowing she was referring to the news about my father. "You know how I felt about the man I thought was my father. I wish my mother hadn't made the choices she did, but I suppose it's what she thought she had to do. What I regret most is not having a chance to know my actual father. How well did you know him?"

"Not too well. Your father chased him off and threatened to raise all kinds of hell. He was a nice man. He was everything your father wasn't. It was easy to see why your mother became involved with him. It was also easy to see why she kept it a secret."

"How did she?"

Out of all the curiosities tumbling about in my thoughts since I'd learned the information my brother and I had always suspected, this question was foremost. Considering both my brother and I had the same father, my mother had kept that relationship a secret for a good three years. Colin was born a year before me. My father was very controlling, so my mother must've gone to great lengths to hide what was happening.

As if she read my mind, Hazel replied,

"Despite your father's controlling tendencies, he wasn't attuned to any emotion other than fear. He was a workaholic, and your mother limited that relationship entirely to work hours. Obviously, he eventually found out, and she ended it immediately and completely."

The regret I couldn't have known I'd experience banged around in my heart. Strangely, the one gift my father had given me was the ability to let go. I didn't learn it from him, but rather from the brutal reality of growing up in a home with a man like him. By the time I was a teenager, I knew quite well the bitterness that came from trying to please someone impossible to please, so I learned to let go.

This regret was different. There was nothing to do to change the events that had taken place. Holding Hazel's gaze, I nodded slowly. "Knowing what my father could do, that makes sense."

Hazel watched me for another moment before reaching over to catch my hand, where it rested on the edge of her desk, and giving it a quick squeeze. "You never were going to be like your father, Ryan. Maybe now you can let that worry go for good."

I lay on the couch in my sitting room with my laptop propped on my legs. I scanned through a spreadsheet Hazel had prepared for me earlier today with comparison data on some investments. My foot moved back and forth, and I glanced down to see Barnable shifting his chin where it rested on my ankle.

"Need something?" I asked.

Barnable's ears perked up. I slid my hand into my pocket and tossed him one of the treats I'd begun carrying in my pocket at all times. He caught it neatly in his mouth. I chuckled to myself. "I hope Addie doesn't mind that I keep giving you treats."

The moment I said her name, I wondered how she was doing. My phone chimed on the coffee table beside the couch. Reaching over, I saw a text from her as if she somehow knew I'd been thinking of her. I doubted that.

My flight leaves tomorrow in the morning. I land at JFK at 5. I wasn't thinking when I got the tickets. It's a terrible time to land. I'll see you whenever I get to your place. Just let me know what time it's ok to come by. Thank you again for watching Barnable.

I tapped out a quick reply.

Don't worry about getting home from the air-

port. I'll have my driver meet you. It's rush hour in New York City. Traffic will be atrocious no matter what you do. Also, stop thanking me for taking care of Barnable. It's my pleasure.

I watch the dots appear and waited for her reply.

You don't have to pick me up, Ryan. You've done more than enough.

I almost replied via text but changed my mind and tapped to call her number.

She picked up immediately. "A phone call?" she said by way of greeting.

"Yes. Are you okay?"

I felt betwixt and between about what to say to Addie. She was there for her father's funeral, and I felt like I was walking in the darkness as to the state of their relationship because she wasn't offering up much.

"I'm fine. I haven't had a chance to tell you much about my family. I'm very close to my mother and her family. So close that I talk to my mother every day no matter where I am. But it wasn't like that with my father. I hardly knew him, and he broke my mother's heart a few too many times when I was younger."

It was almost as if she'd looked into my mind and sensed my curiosity. I absorbed those details and replied carefully, "You hadn't mentioned much about your father, and I didn't want you to think I wasn't thinking about how you were doing."

"Don't get me wrong, his death has stirred some deep waters, but I'm okay. I appreciate you asking."

I wished she were here, so I could see her expression and know how to reply. It wasn't simply her lack of expression that had me proceeding with caution. I didn't really know how to do anything resembling a relationship. In my entire life, my closest relationship had been with my brother, and he was gone. The friendships I had now were all with people I'd known for years. Stepping into something new and so unexpected left me feeling uncertain.

"You don't have to pick me up," she added.

"I'm picking you up, and I'm not arguing about it. Barnable will be disappointed if I don't. We'll have him in the car," I offered, knowing it would probably persuade her.

She laughed softly. "I'll meet you right outside baggage claim and text you when I land."

Chapter Twenty-Six

ADDIE

My mother squeezed me tightly, wrapping me in one of her enveloping hugs. I took a deep breath and squeezed her back before we stepped apart. I let my eyes drift over her familiar face. Her dark hair was streaked with silver and spun into a loose knot, which she held in place with a pencil stabbed through it.

Her dark brown eyes crinkled at the corners when she smiled and lifted her hand to cup my cheek. "I'm so glad you were able to come down for this, dear."

"I wouldn't miss his funeral."

My mother's hand fell away as she turned and lifted a cup of coffee off the kitchen counter. It was early in the morning, and I'd gotten up to enjoy breakfast with her before she took me to the airport. I scanned the familiar kitchen. This was the house where I'd grown up. It was a lovely house tucked in the outskirts of New Orleans.

My mother's kitchen had worn hardwood floors and tall ceilings. A wide window looked out over her backyard, which was in darkness now. I rested my hips against the counter as I sipped my own coffee and waited. Because I knew my mother had something else to say.

My mother curled her hands around her coffee mug and cocked her head to the side. "I didn't assume you would come home for this. I wouldn't have blamed you if you'd chosen not to. You weren't close to your father, and that was entirely his responsibility." My mother's mouth twisted slightly, and bitterness flashed in her eyes.

"It took me a long time to stop hoping for more with him, and I'm sorry for the way it affected you."

My throat tightened with emotion, and I took a swallow of my coffee to move through it. "It's okay. It took me a while to come to terms with the kind of father he was. I'm lucky."

My mother's brows hitched up. "How so?"

"Yes. I have you and our whole family. Not many people can expect to get smothered in love the way I do."

My mother smiled with a soft laugh following. "Smothered might be the way to describe it. You're the best daughter I could've ever imagined, and I'm so proud of you for taking the leap and going to New York City."

Of the many things I loved about my mother, I could add acceptance to that list. Close as she and I were, she fully supported me moving away from New Orleans. She thought it was meant to be that Aunt Eleanor left me her brownstone.

"We'll see how it goes, but I'm glad I'm there," I added with a slight shrug.

"Tell me about this man," my mother commented, her eyes taking on a subtle gleam.

"What man?" I countered quickly, feeling my cheeks heat a bit.

"The one taking care of Barnable for you. You must trust him, or you wouldn't leave your best friend with him," my mother teased.

I took a gulp of my coffee for some fortitude. "I'm not sure. His name is Ryan Blake, and you know how we met."

"How could I forget Barnable's adventure? Well, I sense you like Ryan. I hope you might give him a chance."

"Mama, of course I will," I protested, a sense of defensiveness flaring inside.

One dark brow arched high, and she pursed her lips. "Perhaps, but I worry with you. The one thing that eventually got me to come to my senses about your father was realizing I was unintentionally teaching you the wrong lesson."

"What's that?"

"That not everyone can be trusted. Which is, of course, true. But it's no way to go about approaching romance."

———

Hours and hours later, my mother's words tumbled through my thoughts as I stepped out of the airport doors into the bracing cold evening in New York City. A light mist was falling from the sky. The lights of the city glittered in the rainy darkness.

Ryan had texted me that his driver would be right at the curb. Of course, there were cars everywhere. As my eyes scanned around, I heard my name. Following the sound, I saw Ryan approaching me.

My heart gave a funny little tumble in my

chest. I didn't trust how strongly I reacted to him. All he was doing was walking through the crowd, with confidence and purpose, the way he did basically everything. That was all my body needed to get a little breathless, and for my pulse to take off at a fast gallop.

Ryan stopped in front of me, his eyes sweeping over my face as he reached for my wheeled suitcase at my side.

"Hi. You look like you're freezing." He took my suitcase from me and slid an arm over my shoulders to pull me close.

I instantly wanted to burrow into him. Even through the jacket he wore over what I expected to be a suit, I could feel his heat wrapping itself around me.

Within moments, I was climbing in the backseat of the car and was delighted to find Barnable waiting. Barnable clambered onto my lap and licked my chin. I laughed as I pulled him into my arms and scratched behind his ears the way he liked. "I missed you," I murmured with a kiss on top of his head.

The door on the opposite side opened and closed quickly as Ryan settled in.

"Thank you for bringing Barnable," I said as I smiled over at him.

Ryan's eyes crinkled at the corners as he

smiled at me. "Of course. I knew you'd want to see him right away."

Smitty's voice interjected. "Back to your place, or to Miss Castille's place?"

Ryan looked to me, a question in his eyes.

"Your place if that's okay. I'm not sure if I remembered to turn the heat up, and I'm freezing."

My heart bumped against my ribs as my belly spun in flips. It was a leap for me to state my wish out loud. I wanted to spend the night with Ryan. Emotions had been tumbling through me ever since I'd learned of my father's death. I was craving the closeness, the burn of lust to somehow help me forget.

"My place, Smitty," Ryan replied without ever taking his eyes from mine.

Chapter Twenty-Seven

ADDIE

I was still shivering a little from the damp cold. With my arms crossed, I rubbed my palms up and down while Ryan fed Barnable. A smile curled at the corners of my lips.

"I'm just standing here while you're feeding him. I'm being lazy."

Barnable buried his nose in his food bowl as Ryan straightened and tossed the small plastic measuring cup in Barnable's food bin before snapping the lid over it. Ryan rested his hand on the counter as he looked over at me.

"I wouldn't call it lazy. You just got back from a long flight and..." His words faded as his gaze sobered, and his eyes searched my face. For a moment, I was confused, but then my brain clicked into gear.

"It's okay. You can say it. I wasn't exactly traveling for fun," I offered with a light shrug.

My thoughts had run in circles on the tracks dedicated to my father for the last few days. In many ways, I'd grieved him long ago. Yet, now I had to completely let go. There was no point in wondering if my father would ever regret his almost complete neglect of me beyond anything other than money.

Ryan was quiet for several beats as he studied me before adding, "Yeah, something like that. How are you?"

Such a simple question, yet I wasn't entirely sure of the answer. I was grappling with a sense of finality. I'd also had moments while I was away when I missed Ryan. I didn't know what to make of that. I'd never missed a man in any romantic sense. I missed family and friends but not a man.

My body was reverberating from the little shockwaves of sensation and emotion that Ryan elicited. Tremors of confusion and joy mingled with the hyper-awareness I experienced around him. It was a sensation exclusive to him, as if every cell in my body was attuned to his frequency. There was that, and the desire that just wouldn't quit.

I didn't know if it was appropriate to want someone as fiercely as I wanted him. I didn't know what it meant, but somehow my father's death had created this yearning to connect, to tumble into the intimacy I felt with Ryan. That yearning was so powerful it almost frightened me.

I belatedly realized I hadn't even answered his question. Lifting my chin, I nodded. "I'm okay. Like I told you, I wasn't particularly close to my father."

Ryan nodded slowly, the warmth and understanding held in his eyes almost undoing me. "The reasons might've been different, but I was definitely not close to my father. In some ways, my father's death was a relief, but it was also confusing." Ryan said, his words coming out in careful, measured steps.

The tightness in my chest eased slightly. There was something so, well, sweet about Ryan trying to let me know he understood what I might be going through. It dawned on me that perhaps he understood the confusion I felt more than most would.

"Thank you." My words came out a little raspy. I was tired from the flight and from a lot of talking over the last few days.

"You're cold." I hadn't even noticed I'd wrapped my arms around my waist to try to get warm. He crossed the kitchen toward me, sliding a hand down my back and coaxing me gently. "Let's get you in front of the fire."

I glanced over at Barnable. He'd scarfed down his food in those few short moments of conversation between Ryan and me and was presently curled up on a dog bed I presumed Ryan had purchased for him. He was grooming his feet and clearly content.

I let Ryan lead me down the hallway into the sitting room. Just looking over at the couch with its comfortable cushions and pillows sent a flush through me. It was hard to forget our encounter there last week.

With a flick of a switch, the flames came to life in the gas fireplace, and Ryan tugged me over to the sectional. "The insta-fire is pretty sweet," I commented.

Ryan's quick grin sent butterflies twirling in my belly and heat sliding through my veins as my skin tingled all over. He handed me a soft throw blanket. As I draped it over my lap and settled onto the sofa in front of the fire, he crossed over to the small bar against the wall.

"Something to drink?" he asked.

I'd already declined dinner on the drive

from the airport because I'd eaten during my last layover on the way home. But I wouldn't mind a drink, not one bit. "I'll take a whiskey if you have it," I called over.

"Of course I have whiskey," he murmured softly, a grin teasing at the corners of his mouth.

I watched the flames flickering in the fireplace with the soft sounds of glass clinking and whiskey pouring in the background. In another moment, Ryan was sitting down beside me and handing me a tumbler of whiskey.

"I didn't take you for the type that might prefer whiskey."

I smiled as I took a slow sip. The whiskey slid across my tongue, its flavor rich and mellow. I let out a sigh after I swallowed. "This is delicious, but then, I suppose you have expensive whiskey."

Ryan chuckled as he rested his arm across my shoulders and took a sip from his glass of whiskey. "I don't go cheap."

"What's the whiskey type?" I asked after another swallow, savoring the subtle burn and the way the liquor warmed in my belly.

I angled slightly so I could look up into Ryan's face. When his glacier blue gaze caught mine, the heat radiating from it sent my pulse off like a rocket launch.

Ryan shrugged lightly, his eyes never leaving my face as he took another swallow of whiskey. Dear God. Even his forearms turned me on. I lingered on the subtle flex of the muscles as he tilted the glass up and lowered it.

"I don't know that there's a whiskey type, per se, but not many women like it. Or, if they do, they don't mention it. I should've known you would."

His tone was easy, and his voice low and gravelly. Sparks scattered through my body, and I tried to catch my breath. "Why do you say that?" I managed after a fortifying gulp of whiskey.

"Because you're not like any woman I've ever known, Addie."

He leaned over and set his glass on the coffee table nearby. When he turned to face me again, he brushed a few loose locks of hair off my cheek. The feel of his fingertips dusting over the sensitive skin behind my ear sent shivers rippling through my body, like little earthquakes of sensation.

"Barnable was a good boy," Ryan said softly. "I might have given him too many treats." The sheepish smile that followed his comment had my heart doing cartwheels.

"He's usually a good boy. The worst thing he ever did was break into your basement. Plus, it's impossible to give him too many treats. If you didn't notice, I spoil him rotten."

Ryan's chuckle sent the butterflies into flight again, tickling my belly. I felt as if I were falling from a great height. It felt as if my emotions were pressing against my skin, all of them intense and tangled up with an uncertainty I wasn't ready to examine. Feeling restless and unsettled, I did the only thing that seemed to make a bit of sense in this moment. I leaned up and pressed a kiss on the side of Ryan's neck, the closest place I could reach. Drawing back, I trailed my fingertip along the carved edge of his jaw.

He had an almost aristocratic bend to his features—those angled cheekbones bold and strong, his nose a straight blade if a bit large. It sat so well within the rest of his face and blended together into all too much.

"God was too generous with you," I teased, my voice coming out all breathy.

"Excuse me?"

Leaning back and peering up at him, I

sighed. "You're too handsome for your own good."

Ryan's eyes coasted over my face. Just when I had somehow gotten some purchase in the tumult of my body's intense reaction to him, his hand cupped my cheek, his thumb brushing back and forth across my bottom lip. "I don't know about that, but if God was too generous, it's because I got lucky enough to meet you."

My heart practically burst out of my chest at that with hope throwing pom-poms in the air. I thanked the stars and the universe and then some that Ryan didn't give me much chance to think too hard about what he said. He dipped his head and fit his mouth over mine.

Our kiss spiraled into madness within a matter of seconds. Ryan started out gentle, his mouth fitting softly over mine before he kissed the corners of my lips, and his tongue teased in a slow glide against mine. It was me who felt reckless and restless, frantic to lose myself in the sensation of a passion so over-powering I couldn't think beyond it. There was that and the underlying emotional drum-beat—all the old feelings dredged to the sur-face by my father's death and everything I didn't want to think about.

The way I felt with Ryan was unlike anything I'd ever felt before. Ryan was a gift, and with him, I had a sense of being the only person in the world and also utterly enveloped in his strength. The ability to surrender to the desire rushing through me like a river in spring and feeling more wanted, more *needed* than ever before was intoxicating.

I arched into our kiss, rising up and letting the blanket fall away as I straddled his lap. He was strength and fluidity and my own personal heater. Winding an arm around his shoulders and spearing my fingers in his hair, I melded myself to him as our kiss became hot, wet, and overpowering.

While I might've been the one to pour the gas on this fire, Ryan took control the moment he caught up with me. His tendency to dominate was shockingly pleasurable.

I was always so intent at not letting any man get the upper hand with me, and not ever falling for someone and hoping for more. I always kept myself slightly separate. To be honest, no man had ever affected me powerfully enough in a physical sense to gain an edge.

Except Ryan. With him, the driving heartbeat of our desire mingled with the flashing heat of our chemistry and stripped away my defenses. They burned to ash, and I didn't even care.

I was straddling him and could feel the hard ridge of his arousal against my core. One of his hands gripped my hips, holding me in place as the other slid up my spine to cup my nape and angle my head to the side. I forgot the need to be in control and simply wanted to lose myself in all of this. I didn't want to think about how vulnerable he made me feel when I was able to think.

The sound of Barnable's claws clicking on the hardwood floor and then going quiet as he entered the room distantly pricked my awareness. Ryan broke free from our kiss, his head falling back against the cushions.

Our breath came in ragged gasps. I felt Barnable's nose nudge one of my feet, and I glanced over my shoulder to see him eyeing us curiously.

Ryan's low laugh rumbled in his chest, and I felt the vibration in my own body. I was already suffused with heat from head to toe, and my cheeks got hotter as I glanced back at him. "We have an audience."

"I don't mind the interruption, but I'm fucking you properly tonight."

His low, blunt, slightly dirty words sent a

thrill through me. I was already slick at my core, but I became acutely aware of it, and my hips rocked restlessly over his hot length.

Ryan bit his lip as he watched me, but he stayed silent. My heartbeat was hammering so hard I could feel every beat reverberating through my body, echoing while blood rushed through my ears.

Ryan stood, lifting me easily against him. I reflexively curled my legs around his hips as he adjusted me in his arms. Without ever looking away, he reached to the side and tapped the button to turn off the fire.

"We're going to my bedroom."

"Okay," I said breathlessly as he began walking.

Barnable began to follow us, his trot well known to my ears as Ryan strode down the hallway. He called over his shoulder, "You're not coming with us, Barnable."

I was one of those people who thought dogs understood language better than humans believed. Once again, Barnable proved my point. When Ryan turned to start walking up the stairs at the front of the house, Barnable reversed direction. By the sounds of it, he returned to the kitchen where his dog bed was.

"I'm not much for an audience," Ryan said, his voice husky.

I giggled and couldn't resist leaning down to breathe in the scent of him. I nipped lightly at his neck.

He squeezed my bottom where he held me firmly with one hand. "We're getting all the way to the bedroom, so don't push it."

I giggled again, and my heart pounded away. Although I couldn't even contemplate trying to deny the fact that pure, raw, and downright ferocious lust was a driving factor in this moment, my heart knew there was so much more to it.

It felt all too good to be with Ryan. As vulnerable as I felt, I also felt as if I could be entirely myself. So, I leaned forward and nipped again, a little thrill chasing through me when he growled as we crested the top stair.

"Payback is coming," he murmured when I leaned back. My pussy clenched at his words.

In seconds, he was shouldering through a doorway, lights coming on low instantly. They began to brighten until Ryan said, "Dim."

The lights immediately dimmed again, and I stared at him, my eyes wide as he lowered me onto the foot of his bed. "Wow, even your lights do what you tell them."

"They do. Now it's your turn to do what I say."

He rested his hands beside my hips, caging me between his arms. His presence could have felt overwhelming. Instead, I savored the strength emanating from him and the feeling of being wholly encompassed in his heat and power.

I licked my lips while I tried to get a breath. I managed nothing more than a shallow sip of air. I couldn't keep from shifting my thighs, restless to relieve the ache between them. I could feel my swollen, slick folds slide when I moved.

Ryan didn't say a word, although his icy blue eyes darkened slightly. I took another breath. "Okay," I rasped on my exhalation.

"That's my girl," Ryan murmured in return, the promise contained in his words sending a fiery hot shiver racing through my body.

He straightened, his eyes sweeping up and down my body where I was sitting on the end of his bed. "Clothes off."

He stepped back as he shrugged out of his suit jacket and tossed it to the side where it landed on a chair nearby. My breath caught in my throat as he began to unbutton his shirt, revealing a dusting of dark hair on his chest, his bronze skin gleaming in the dim light when his shirt fell open.

I hadn't realized I was simply sitting there with my mouth falling open until he leveled me with his gaze. "This isn't a one-man show."

His words and the dirty look in his eyes made my pussy clench. I snapped my mouth shut and shimmied off the bed. Within seconds, I was down to my panties and bra. I was just reaching to undo the clasp between my breasts when Ryan stepped closer, his hand curling over mine. "Save that for me."

My heart was beating madly like a trapped bird. I looked up toward him, my eyes soaking in the sight of his sculpted chest and traveling downward. He was fully naked, his cock curving upward, thick and erect.

My eyes finally made their way up to meet Ryan's, and then impossibly, my heart beat even faster. There was a rushing sensation inside, a force I couldn't contain.

Our breath moved in tune with one another. *In and out. In and out. In and out.*

It felt as if he were actually making love to me with his eyes alone. His hand was still curled around mine, with his knuckles resting against my breastbone. I could hardly bear the intensity and intimacy.

Ryan finally broke the spell when he released my hand. His palms slid down my sides, caressing the dip at my waist before easing over my hips. Everything began to blur. He lifted me onto the bed and stretched out beside me. It felt as if we were operating in a suspended place and time where nothing but desire, need, and sensation reigned.

Ryan's hands mapped my body, finding every place to touch. The gentle brush of his thumb across a nipple, the firm sweep of his palm over my bottom, the scrape of his teeth on my neck. My breasts were heavy and aching as he cupped one and the other, drawing my nipples, one at a time, into the warm suction of his mouth. The hot brand of his cock pressing against my skin and then cradled between my thighs.

I cried out when he shifted down, his tongue trailing a teasing path over my belly. His palms pressed my knees apart, and he licked into me. Sensation scattered through me, and I heard myself crying out incoherently as he took his sweet time. He brought me to the edge again and again with his tongue and fingers, only letting me topple over when I begged. Pleasure poured through me in rough tremors.

While my release was still rippling, Ryan rose up over me, his weight settling down carefully.

"Look at me, Addie."

My eyelids were heavy, but I managed to drag them open. I found his gaze waiting, hot and intent. He rocked into me, his shaft sliding easily through my swollen folds, soaked with the juices of my arousal.

I almost came again at the subtle pressure over my clit. I heard myself gasping his name again. I'd never begged a man in my life, but I was beyond shame. Any inhibition I had was long gone, melted into the fire swirling around us and catching us in its flames.

His crown nudged at my entrance. "Please..." I begged. Again.

"Addie." The sound of my name in Ryan's taut voice brought my eyes open again. "I want to see you."

His strong body vibrated from the tension as he held himself above me. I savored the weight of him, the feel of every muscle against my skin.

All of a sudden, he shook his head swiftly. "Condom," he bit out.

I couldn't make sense of why, but I

wanted to feel him, all of him with no barriers between us. Although I didn't trust my own heart, I trusted him in this.

He began to move back, but I curled my legs around and held him in place. "No need. I'm on the pill. Not because I'm busy," I explained hurriedly. "It's just I have been for years."

Ryan held perfectly still, his eyes searching mine.

"Are you sure?"

"I trust you."

"It's your call," he said after we breathed together for several more heartbeats.

"I need you."

Chapter Twenty-Eight

RYAN

I need you.

Addie's words echoed as I looked into her eyes. I was barely, and I do mean barely, in control.

I was hanging on the face of a cliff, and my grip was sliding. I could feel the kiss of her slick core. The fierce need to be joined with her ran so deep I could feel it in my bones.

"Ryan." My name in Addie's voice was like sorghum sliding over me, the sweetness slipping like smoke through the remaining cracks in the defenses around my heart.

Her hips rocked against me, and I slid into her in one deep stroke, burying myself to the hilt immediately. Addie held my gaze the entire time, and my heart pounded with such force, every beat strained the bones of my ribs.

Being buried inside of her was a pleasure beyond intoxicating. I held still, my release nearly coming at the feel of her channel rippling around my length. Her hips rocked again, just a little nudge into mine.

I'd meant to take control of this, to seduce away Addie's defenses with my hands, my lips, my tongue, my teeth, and my need. Addie was *mine*. I set out to show her that tonight.

And yet, I underestimated the power she held over me simply in being who she was. I could tell earlier tonight she was out of sorts and a bit unsettled. With her crooked smile and glittering eyes, everything about her was so pure. In that, she took all ability to calculate away from me.

My body moved on its own with my hips shifting back. I slid into her again, the friction between us keeping me right at the edge. My efforts to maintain some control spun into the force itself.

Our encounter was slow and sensual in the dim light of my bedroom, a room no other woman had ever been in. That was too personal. Yet, I couldn't wait to get Addie here in my bed with me twisted like vines that couldn't be separated.

I felt Addie quicken as her breath became more ragged, and her walls rippled tightly around my cock with each stroke into her, notching deeper every time. Her fingers tightened where our hands were joined right before she let out a rough shout with my name following.

My own release came almost instantly, a lash at the base of my spine sending electricity jolting upward as my balls tightened. I let go, my release pouring into her.

The sound of our breathing filled the air around us as I rolled us over. Addie shifted to slide to my side, but I didn't want to lose our connection just yet. I held her tight.

"Oh no, you don't," I murmured into the curtain of her hair that had fallen across my face.

She fell against me, all soft curves and dewy skin. This would be the time I would typically find a way to gracefully but efficiently untangle myself and leave. But I didn't usually bring anyone into my space, and I didn't want Addie to leave. Not at all.

As I felt the beat of her heart slow in tune with mine, she rose up, resting her hand on my chest and curling it into a soft fist. Her eyes searched my face. She had emotionally bulldozed me, and I had no idea what to say. I waited quietly.

Before Addie, I had mastered the art of keeping people at bay, most particularly women who might want anything more than casual from me. I sensed I'd tumbled into love by accident. Yet, I didn't think Addie was quite there yet.

I didn't know all the pieces of the puzzle that told the story inside her heart. I knew she was guarded and vulnerable, and I was going to have to win her over.

As my heart pounded away, its beat right and true because its owner was skin to skin with me, Addie's lips curled in a slow smile. "You're too much," she announced.

My own smile came automatically. Because it was almost impossible not to smile when Addie did. Her smiles were too pure, too genuine.

"Oh?"

She bit her lip and nodded before pressing a kiss to my jaw. A little spiral of heat radiated outward from that tiny point of contact.

"Yes," she said with an elaborate sigh. "You're handsome, you're sexy, and you're wealthy. You're also ridiculously good in bed."

My laugh rumbled up from my chest. "I'm guessing you don't care about much of any of that."

Addie shook her head, her cheeks tingeing pink. "You're too easy on the eyes for me to complain about your looks. I'd be lying if I didn't say you could probably keep me as your personal sex slave, and I wouldn't complain."

———

The following morning, I woke after the best sleep of my entire life. Which was saying something because, in hours, I didn't get very much sleep. But the quality of the sleep I did get was thorough. After we started the night, Addie insisted she needed a snack in bed. We fell asleep after she made a plate of cheese and crackers for us.

We woke twice more during the night, our hands finding each other again and again. As the hours ticked by, we made love in the sleepy haze of darkness.

Addie insisted on making pancakes for breakfast. We lounged at the kitchen table while we enjoyed coffee, and Barnable napped at our feet. After I drained my coffee,

I set my empty mug on the table and idly traced a circle around the base of it.

Addie was doing the daily crossword puzzle. I kept the habit of getting a paper delivered because I liked the tactile experience of flipping through it while I had coffee before I left for the office in the mornings.

"Do you always do the daily crossword?"

Addie finished whatever word she was filling in and glanced over at me. She smiled slightly. "I do. I like word games."

We stared at each other for a long moment, and I became aware of the resounding beat of my heart.

Addie's eyes broke from mine first as a pretty pink flush crested on her cheeks. I wanted to eat her up.

"What is a basis for comparison?" she asked as she picked up her pencil again and studied the puzzle.

"A measure, perhaps."

Addie quickly penciled it in and cast a bright smile at me. "That's it." She smoothed her palm over the paper and folded it before reaching up to spin her hair into a knot. She stuck the pencil through it to hold it in place.

Her eyes shifted to the clock mounted on the wall above the archway into the kitchen. "Aren't you going into work?"

I had to take a deep breath to breathe through the tightness clenching around my heart. "I am, and I'm late. Hazel will have something to say about that," I offered with a wry grin.

Addie laughed as she stood from her chair. "I actually need to get home to do some work. I've got a few drawings to turn in for some cards by the end of this week, and I'm a little behind schedule because of my trip."

Reluctant didn't even capture how I felt about letting this morning end. I stood with her. "I definitely need to get to the office."

"Is it okay if I run upstairs and grab my things?"

"Of course."

Addie turned and walked quickly across the room. I gave myself a mental shake and crossed over to the kitchen counter to fetch my phone. As I was replying to a text from Hazel to let her know I would be in the office shortly, a call came in.

I accidentally answered it. Not because I intended to, but rather because smartphones weren't always that smart. My thumb was moving down to type a letter when it switched into the call mode for the incoming call. I hadn't even seen who was calling. Considering the very short list of people who had my personal number, I figured I could easily deal with it.

"Hello."

"Hi, Ryan. How are you? You rarely answer, so I feel lucky this morning."

I bit back a sigh. Marla Clark was definitely not someone I would've chosen to speak with. She legitimately had my personal number. That was because I gave it to her before I realized she didn't have a clear understanding of how defined my boundaries were with regard to romance.

I knew Marla socially through business. She ran in the same business circles and was VP of operations for her father's investment company. We'd gone on a few business dates to functions. Then, she made her interest in something more than that clear.

I'd immediately drawn back. It had been several months since I'd seen her.

"Good morning, Marla. You might feel lucky, but to be honest, I was in the middle of a text and accidentally answered." I felt my cynical, snarky side rise up quickly. I had little patience for flirting games.

Marla giggled coquettishly in my ear, and I rolled my eyes. "What can I do for you?"

"Since we're being honest, I'd like to clear the air."

"I only have a few minutes."

"We have something, Ryan. I can respect that you don't want to do the whole song and dance around romance, but we have chemistry, the sex is great, and we understand each other. I thought I would just cut to the chase since you've been avoiding me. Let's enjoy what we have. If you want to reconsider and move towards marriage, let's look at it as a business arrangement."

I was glad she wasn't here to see my face because my mouth fell open. It was hard to surprise me, but Marla had most assuredly done that. I collected my thoughts before replying. "Marla, I think I already made myself clear, but apparently I need to repeat myself. I'm not interested in anything serious. Not romance, nor your proposed business marriage."

Chapter Twenty-Nine

ADDIE

I'm not interested in anything serious. Not romance, nor your proposed business marriage.

Ryan's words had played like a broken record through my thoughts for days now. No matter how hard I tried to nudge the needle onto a different track, it kept skipping back.

I'd been walking down the hallway toward the kitchen after fetching my purse and jacket. I'd been floating on the high of our night together and feeling rather emotionally raw. Perhaps it was a result of the unsettled emotions stirred by my father's death. Or, perhaps it was because I'd let my guard down and it felt so good.

For what felt like the thousandth time, I forced my thoughts off of Ryan. I had a deadline for work, and I needed to stay focused. I sketched quickly, but I was distracted, and it was hard to lose myself in the project. Although I'd always loved to draw when I was young, even I'd been surprised at how quickly I'd fallen in love with designing greeting cards. Although it was a commercial type of art, it was fun, quirky, and sometimes silly.

The flexibility of it had allowed me to move to New York City. Although it took more time than usual, I managed to complete several draft ideas and send them off. Restless and needing something to distract me from obsessing about Ryan and what an idiot I'd been, I wished I had a friend to call or visit.

Impulsively, I texted Soraya. While we weren't that close yet, I liked her and felt like I could talk to her. I was practically ecstatic when she replied and invited me to stop by.

I glanced down at Barnable. "Do you want to go see Soraya?" I asked.

One of his ears stood up as he looked up at me for a moment with his body wiggling back and forth. "I'll take that as a yes."

After I got his sweater on, which I wasn't so sure he liked, I buttoned my down coat and wound my scarf around my neck before we stepped out. I walked Barnable several times a day and was getting to know my neighborhood. There were a few other dog walkers who reliably waved to me now, which made me feel like I was starting to be a part of the community here. I headed over to a route I liked to take in the park. Barnable was well behaved as long as he had plenty of exercise. I wanted him to be on his best behavior at Soraya's.

He trotted along at my side, stopping to do his business along the way. I disposed of the doggy bag in one of the marked places specifically for dog waste. I was just about to head back toward the address Soraya had texted me when I heard my name. My heart twisted in my chest, and my throat tightened.

Ryan had texted and even called over the last few days. Every time, I brushed him off with, in all honesty, lame excuses. For the first time in the last few days, I was relieved to hear his words echo in my mind. No matter what I thought I felt that night, Ryan wasn't interested in more. It would serve me well to keep that foremost in my mind.

On the heels of a deep breath, I turned. Ryan was only a few feet away, and everything inside me froze for a moment. Why did I have to feel so much for him?

It didn't help matters for Barnable to get all excited and start wiggling like crazy when he saw Ryan approaching. He even let out one of his little happy barks. I tried to keep my expression passive and polite when Ryan stopped in front of us.

"Addie," he said when he stopped. "I—" His eyes flicked down when Barnable nudged him demandingly against his calf.

"Hey, buddy," he said, his voice warming as he leaned down to pet Barnable. Glancing back up to me, Ryan grinned. "I couldn't bring myself to put the sweater on him while you were gone."

My heart was racing along in a jumbled beat. I did *not* need to think Ryan was a great guy just because he liked my dog. He could like my dog and still not want romance.

I wasn't going to repeat history. My mother had longed for a man who was never available and had only come to her senses years later. I refused to let myself go there. So what if Ryan and I had amazing sex? It was just sex.

I pasted a tight smile on my face.

The lines of tension on his face were obvious, and I could practically feel the concern in his eyes. I steeled myself to withstand the effect he would have on my body. I felt like a cat wanting to purr and lean into someone's touch. A sharp gust of cold, winter wind blew by, brushing my hair against my cheeks.

Ryan searched my face. "Is everything okay?"

"It's fine. I've just been busy." I hoped my tone sounded casual because that was what I was aiming for.

He looked at me quietly, and I felt as if he could see right into me. I wanted to close the shutters to my heart and soul to hold him at bay. I feared they'd been blown off the hinges the other night.

"Are you sure? I understand busy. I'd still love to take you out for dinner."

Sometimes I hated my tendency to blurt out the truth. What happened next only re-inforced how annoyed I could get with myself.

"I don't think we should go to dinner again, Ryan. I think maybe I'm not your type."

Ryan stepped closer, his gaze nearly searing me and sending my pulse lunging. "Addie, you're the only woman who is my type."

I wanted to cry, right then and there. I thanked God for my stubbornness because I clung to my pride and lifted my chin. "I don't think so. You can take this however you'd like, and I wasn't trying to eavesdrop, but I overheard you the other morning right before I left. 'No romance.' I understand. That's what I would've expected from you. I was foolish enough to let myself think otherwise. I don't know how to do things like that, and I really like you, which isn't smart. I want to believe I can learn from my mistakes, so that's what I'm doing now. I really do appreciate you helping me when Barnable broke into your basement and helping me find a new attorney. They haven't sent a bill over, so I'll make sure to call and reimburse anything you paid. I don't want you to think I owe you anything."

I stopped then, my words running out along with my breath. I felt shaky and tingly all over—regret, confusion, and frustration spinning tightly inside.

Ryan's eyes had gone wide. He started to reach for one of my hands, but I stepped back quickly and curled both hands tightly around Barnable's leash. As if holding onto that could save me.

Ryan closed his eyes, and his shoulders rose and fell with a breath. When he opened his eyes again, I could've sworn I saw regret and hurt flashing in the depths. I definitely saw determination because his jaw tightened, and he squared his shoulders.

"Addie, it's not what you think. I was making that clear to someone I have no interest in. It's not like that with you."

Hope was beating tiny fists on the door of the closet where I'd locked it deep in my heart. I ignored it. "Ryan, you don't need to make me promises you can't keep. You can't even understand how much this hits a sore spot for me. I wasn't close to my father because he was never around. He was wealthy, and I was nothing more than an accident to him." I closed my eyes and swallowed through the emotion clogging my throat. When I opened them again, I could see Ryan was listening intently, waiting for me to finish.

"My mother pined for him for years, and I was the little girl who always wondered where her father was. I eventually understood, and my mother finally stopped wishing for something that would never be. But I promised myself I was never going to fall for a man who didn't want what I did. I don't want you to make an exception for me. I won't lie. The sex is incredible, and I almost tricked myself into thinking it meant something more. But it's just sex."

Ryan opened his mouth to say something, but I shook my head quickly. "Just let me go."

I didn't wait for his reply and turned away, walking swiftly with Barnable trotting at my side.

Chapter Thirty

RYAN

"Excuse me," I snapped as I walked quickly away from a woman who approached me at a business function for investors in a real estate planning consortium.

Unfortunately, I'd made the mistake of deciding to attend this solo and was finding myself annoyed at being approached by women. I hadn't been able to bring myself to invite anyone to accompany me. I missed Addie, and it felt like a betrayal to her.

Even though she'd cut me out. Just thinking about her was like a knife, its blade jagged, being dragged across the surface of my heart.

Striding to the bar, I ordered a scotch. I

felt a presence beside me and glanced over to find Graham. "How's it going?" he asked.

Graham's question was perfectly normal and polite, but I could tell by the knowing look in his eyes that he sensed I was out of sorts. The bartender handed over my drink, and I passed across a twenty-dollar bill, telling him to keep the change.

After a quick gulp of the smooth scotch, I looked toward Graham again. "I'm fine. Yourself?"

"I'm well. I was expecting to see you with Addie tonight."

Graham's mention of Addie was another drag of that jagged knife blade across my aching heart. I took a breath and shrugged. After another gulp of my scotch, which I couldn't even enjoy, I replied, "Addie and I aren't seeing each other anymore."

Graham's eyes widened slightly. "Sorry to hear that. I liked her."

At that moment, Soraya approached, stopping beside Graham and leaning up to press a kiss on his cheek. The love between them was an almost palpable force. Graham glanced down to her, his gaze softening immediately. I was confident he completely forgot where they were. He literally had eyes only for her.

"Hi, I wasn't sure you were going to make it." He leaned down and caught her lips in a lingering kiss.

Soraya's mouth curled into a smile when he drew back. As usual, she was stunning. With her dark hair swept up in an elegant knot, she wore a white dress that set off her gorgeous skin. Although Soraya wasn't like Addie, she brought Addie to my thoughts instantly. Mostly because she wasn't anything like the bland beauties who tended to run in business circles. Soraya was decidedly herself, with her strong personality and bold beauty.

"Of course I made it. Just running a little late." She glanced my way. "Nice to see you, Ryan. Is Addie here tonight?"

Yet another drag of the knife across my heart. I'd honestly never understood the concept of heartbreak. I feared, in my case, it was going to be death by a thousand cuts. My heart was being shredded bit by bit since losing Addie.

Graham graciously answered for me, almost as if he sensed my pain. "Apparently, they're not seeing each other anymore." Graham's gaze landed on mine. "You should know Soraya thought Addie may have the ability to steal your heart."

Soraya's eyes searched my face. I was discovering I didn't like feeling vulnerable.

"I saw her the other day. I walked Blackie with her and her dog, and we had coffee."

"Barnable," I said, unable to keep from smiling at the thought of Addie's dog.

"I told Addie about Tig," Soraya said, looking toward Graham. "She wants to get her tattoo repaired."

I actually had to bite the inside of my cheek to keep from asking more. What Addie did was none of my damn business. I took another gulp of my scotch, draining the glass.

"Are you okay?" Soraya asked when she looked back at me.

Fuck it. Considering that I had absolutely no clue how to handle the situation with Addie, I figured I might as well ask. "Not really. I actually liked Addie. A lot. She thinks I'm a bad bet."

Graham stayed quiet, but Soraya reached a hand out, gently squeezing my elbow. "Oh, I'm so sorry. I thought you two were good together. What happened?"

"Unfortunately, she overheard me when I got a call from Marla, you remember her?"

Graham rolled his eyes. "Oh yes. Marla, who's always looking for a husband?"

"That's the one. All Addie heard was me telling Marla I wasn't interested in romance. Which is true when it comes to anyone other than Addie," I said, my words coming out sharp. "Honestly, I don't know what the fuck to do. I probably am a bad bet."

"No, you're not," Soraya said firmly. "You just need to figure out how to fight for Addie."

I rolled my head from side to side, trying to ease the tension bundling in my neck. "I have no fucking clue what to do."

A sly smile curled Graham's lips. "You should write to Ask Ida. She's usually got pretty direct advice."

Soraya laughed. "Maybe you should, you never know what she'll say."

————

Dear Ida,

I've never been interested in romance. In fact, I didn't think I would ever fall in love. Turns out I was wrong. I met someone. She's nothing like any woman I've ever met. Her dog was lost, and she was trying to break in my basement. That turned out to be the best thing that ever happened to me.

For a few weeks, I thought I had a chance. I don't know what to do because she doesn't think I'm worth it. There was a misunderstanding, and she thinks I don't want anything serious. I'd do anything to get her back, but relationships aren't exactly my thing. In fact, my experience in this category is a big fat zero. Any advice you could offer about how to convince her I'm worth it would be great.

Regards,
Clueless in New York

Chapter Thirty-One

RYAN

Ida, unfortunately, didn't answer me immediately, and I felt like a fucking idiot after hitting send on that email. I'd been reduced to writing in to an advice column about my love life. Fuck my life.

After growing up in the long shadow cast by my parents' cold and miserable marriage and dealing with the grief of my brother, it had seemed easy to decide I wasn't interested in romance, or love. Right about now, it felt as if the universe was having a hearty laugh at my expense.

All this time, I'd thought my biggest challenge would be keeping it clear that I wasn't interested in romance to all the women out there who were fortune hunters, or otherwise interested in the elaborate fantasy of happily ever after. If one single lesson had been burned into my brain like a brand made by ice, it was the lesson of my parents' marriage. For years, I hadn't believed love was even possible.

Apparently, the universe was here to show me how wrong I'd been. I was flat out in love with Adelaide Castille, and I couldn't get her to answer a text or return a phone call. For a man accustomed to feeling in control, this was an uncomfortably novel situation for me. Feelings were messy, and I didn't like it.

Fuck, fuck, fuck.

In an effort to welcome any and all distractions, I accepted an invite from Graham to grab drinks one evening after work. Well, not after my work, because I'd once again resumed my ridiculous schedule of working during all of my waking hours.

Despite my best efforts at staying too distracted to think about Addie or dwell on the constant ache in my heart, my snide, cynical voice was ready and quick.

See, all these years, you convinced yourself you just loved work.

Fuck off, I mentally countered.

My snide voice was well-honed and reeled

off another jab. *The truth hurts, doesn't it? All this time, you've been a master at avoiding everything and everyone who mattered.*

My repertoire of retorts was limited. *Fuck off.* My quieter voice was a little louder this time.

All I got in return for this mental series of volleys was a sly laugh.

When I stepped out of my office building, after casting a glare over at the office of the attorney who'd been an ass to Addie, snow was falling lightly. My mind instantly conjured an image of Addie's eyes wide with wonder as she looked up when snow started falling from the sky a few weeks ago.

With it being dark tonight, the fluffy snowflakes glittered under the streetlights, melting as they met the pavement and concrete. I walked briskly to the bar where Graham had asked me to meet him. It was a rather exclusive place.

Shouldering through the door, I didn't even have to flash my ID to get in. People mostly knew who I was around here. Graham lifted his hand from where he sat at a small round table in the corner by the windows. My footsteps were muted on the carpet as I crossed the room to where he was.

I slipped into the chair directly across

from him. "Hi there," I said as I shrugged out of my jacket and let it fall over the back of my chair.

"How's it going?" Graham asked. He nodded toward a glass of scotch already on the table in front of me. "I took the liberty of ordering your preferred scotch."

"Thank you." I lifted the scotch with one hand as I smoothed my other hand over my hair, which was damp from the snow falling outside.

Graham was quiet as I took several swallows of my drink. After I set my glass down, he asked, "Hungry?"

I shrugged. I was hungry in the technical sense of probably needing food for sustenance. But I'd had hardly any appetite over the last few days. I missed Addie, and the feeling ran to my bones. Nothing felt right. I couldn't even believe my emotional state was affecting my physical state. Yet, I couldn't deny it, not even to myself. "Might as well eat."

Graham lifted his hand, catching the attention of a waiter. After the waiter swung by our table and took our orders, Graham cocked his head to the side as he studied me.

"You look fucking miserable," he observed.

I rolled my eyes. "Why the hell do you say that?" I heard a hint of defensiveness in my tone and was almost shocked. I was prone to not giving a fuck what anybody thought. Yet, Graham was so spot on it was like another sharp slice to the heart where it hurt the most.

I took a deep breath and closed my eyes as I let it out. I didn't need to be an ass to Graham. He was actually a friend. I was relieved to see the waiter approaching when I opened my eyes. I drained the last bit of my scotch and handed him my empty glass as he sat down two fresh drinks.

"Thank you," Graham said as the waiter spun away.

Graham was patient enough to wait me out because he knew me that well. After a swallow of my scotch and another deep breath, I inclined my head. "Apologies. I'm being an ass."

"Hazel mentioned you've been irritable when I called earlier. That's what prompted my invite to drinks. I wasn't sure you'd take me up on it." A smile teased at the corners of his mouth as he regarded me.

"I'm sure I haven't been at my best at the office. It's Addie. She dumped me," I said flatly, a sense of relief rolling through me at simply being direct with my friend.

"Yeah, you mentioned that the other night." I was so unsettled with missing Addie, I barely recalled telling Graham and Soraya we weren't seeing each other anymore. "I didn't know you were getting serious about her. I thought you were, but I wasn't sure," Graham said slowly.

"I don't know if we were either, but it doesn't matter now. She doesn't consider me a good bet."

Graham lifted his glass, watching the light glint off the rich amber liquid as he swirled the glass in his palm. He met my eyes, understanding flickering in his. "Love isn't a bet, Ryan." He rarely spoke of it, but he'd been burned badly by his ex who screwed around on him with his best friend. What he'd found with Soraya had surprised him as much as those who knew him and the bitterness he'd carried over that old betrayal.

I stared at him. "I don't suppose it is." I chuckled softly, laughing at myself.

Graham was quiet for several beats before he shrugged lightly. "I could've missed my chance with Soraya if I'd let my past get in the way. What do you mean Addie thinks you're a bad bet? Is that what she said?"

"No. That's my interpretation. Like I mentioned the other night, Addie overheard what I said to Marla."

"What the hell did you say?" Graham countered with a pointed look.

"I told Marla I wasn't interested in romance or marriage. Hearing it now, I realized how bad it could've sounded to Addie."

Graham shook his head slowly. "Yeah, not a great thing for her to overhear. I like Addie. I actually thought she would be good for you."

"She is. I just have to convince her I'm good for her."

"You've never failed at something you set your mind to. I think this time you're going to have to take a different approach."

———

Dear Clueless in New York City,

My advice to you is simple. If you want this woman, fight for her. Don't be an idiot and hope she can read between the lines. Be direct, be honest, and lay your cards on the table.

I sense you're not a man accustomed to being vulnerable. The only way to win her heart is to open yours. This is not a business deal. You can't do a pros and cons list and assess a balance sheet. You're going to have to take a risk and see what happens. I wish you all the best and lots of luck.

Ida

p.s. Be a fool in love.

Chapter Thirty-Two

ADDIE

Barnable's body started vibrating as he wagged all over and bounced lightly on his front feet. I knew without even looking ahead that Ryan was approaching us. My hairs stood up like tiny antennas all over my body turning to face him.

My heart was achy, and I'd been irritable over the last week or more while I ignored his texts and phone calls. I needed to be a more modern girl and appreciate the incredible orgasms I'd never forget from our interludes. Instead, my emotions were swamping me, and I missed him so much it was a physical pain.

Barnable even let out a little yelp of excitement. I finally looked ahead to see Ryan was only about ten feet away on the sidewalk. I tightened my grip on Barnable's leash. I wanted to tell myself that was because I needed to make sure I had a firm grip, but that would've been a big fat lie. Barnable's leash was my anchor in the maelstrom of emotion spinning through me.

I pasted a polite smile on my face and ignored the way my pulse took off when Ryan stopped in front of me. Why did he have to go and be so damn handsome? His cheeks were ruddy from the cold winter day. As usual, since it was a workday, Ryan wore a suit. He had an overcoat that wasn't even buttoned over it. I could see the way everything caressed the muscled planes of his body like an appreciative lover. It wouldn't surprise me to learn Ryan had his suits tailored. Considering that I'd grown up sewing, I was confident his tailor would appreciate just how amazing a suit could look on Ryan. There were tricks you could do with fabric, but nothing could do better than a natural form such as Ryan's.

He was a sculptor's dream. I silently swatted this train of thought away as heat bloomed from my core outward. I had a vivid recollection of the feel of his body as he came down over me.

Dead last on the list of things I should be thinking about right now was the way it felt to have Ryan stretch my channel. I definitely didn't need to experience the pleasure pinging through my body at nothing more than a memory.

Ryan's eyes searched my face. He didn't speak at first, yet my heart felt as if his eyes communicated pain and uncertainty. I wanted to reach out and hug him and tell him it would all be okay. Yet, I needed not to be foolish.

Barnable yelped again, and Ryan tore his eyes from mine to lean over and greet him. "Hey, buddy." The low, melodic sound of his voice stung the raw surface of my heart.

As soon as he straightened, he said, "Addie, please talk to me."

A man's elbow hit me abruptly as he walked by, and Ryan stepped closer, sheltering me with his arm. I wanted to lean into him, and tears stung at the backs of my eyes.

"Just have dinner with me," he urged.

Another body bumped into me, and Ryan swore. "Fuck. No one slows down."

"Well, we are standing on the sidewalk in downtown Manhattan, and it's around lunchtime," I said, managing a wry smile.

"Please, Addie."

The urge to say "yes" nearly overwhelmed me, but I pushed back against it. I shook my head quickly. "I can't. I have to go."

I didn't wait for Ryan's reply, and I felt like a coward as I hurried past him, almost yanking poor Barnable along with me. Barnable caught up quickly, shifting from a walk to his bouncy jog. I did actually have somewhere to be. I was meeting Soraya for coffee and tea.

I was relieved I didn't have too far to walk. After I dropped Barnable off at home, I was still feeling rattled when I hurried into the coffee shop where I was meeting Soraya. My heart was thumping erratically, and my breath was still shallow.

Soraya glanced up, a smile stretching across her face when I stopped beside the table where she was waiting. "Hey, you made it."

"Of course. Should I get in line, or do they check on tables here?" I asked, noticing she already had a mug in front of her.

Soraya closed her laptop and gestured at the chair across from her. "They'll stop by the table."

I slipped into the chair and shrugged my jacket off my shoulders as I looked around the café. It had a cozy feel to it with small, circular tables scattered through the space, a wide wooden counter that ran the length of the back wall with a display case of bakery items and whatnot, and a large chalkboard with a menu of drinks and food above.

"Have you had lunch yet?" Soraya asked.

I shook my head. The truth was I hadn't had much of an appetite lately. I was so off-kilter with this whole Ryan thing. For the most part in life, I knew who I was and didn't care to try to fit any mold. I didn't worry about fitting in and so on. But I'd have happily bargained with the devil to be more casual about men and relationships. I'd never done the whole casual sex thing easily. While I was no innocent, I had to guard against falling hard and fast. The tricky thing about trust issues is the very people who have trouble with trust often desperately want to be proven wrong. That was me, always wishing for more despite my deeply ingrained cynicism about love. As a result, I'd skirted away from dating ever since a brief college relationship had taught me some brutal lessons. There was that, and my promise to myself to never be like my mother.

Yet, I couldn't stop thinking about Ryan after only two nights with him. Ugh. Even though he was persistent in asking me to talk, I seriously doubted he was obsessing over me the way I was over him. I wanted to be a modern girl who could handle something casual and who could take the orgasms for the awesome thing they were and carry on.

I hadn't realized I'd let my mind wander onto the track of Ryan in my brain until Soraya spoke. "Addie? Are you okay?"

"Oh! Sorry. Just zoned out. I'm fine, and I should probably eat something."

Just then, a waitress with her hair in two braids stopped by, casting a sunny smile between us. "Anything to drink?"

"Coffee, please. Dark and no cream," I said.

Soraya handed me a small menu. "Order some food."

While Soraya ordered a sandwich, I quickly scanned the menu. "I'll take the cream of broccoli soup with the fresh bread," I said when the waitress looked toward me again.

"Got it. Be back in a few with your coffee." She hurried off, her braids swinging as she walked away.

Moments later, I took a few sips of my coffee, savoring the warmth after coming in from the blustery cold day. "Oh, this is good," I commented.

Soraya sighed. "I know. They have the best coffee here."

"Aren't you having some?"

Soraya flushed slightly before shaking her head. "It's tea for me." She paused before adding, "I'm pregnant. We're only now telling people because I'm past the first trimester."

"Oh wow! Congratulations! That's wonderful news."

Soraya nodded. "We're pretty excited. While I miss coffee, I'm eating like a crazy person." She paused, eyeing me for a moment. "Now, tell me what's wrong."

I sputtered on my sip of coffee and reached for a napkin to dab at my mouth. Soraya waited patiently.

"What do you mean?" I finally asked.

"I know we haven't known each other too long, but when I saw you come in, you looked like you were about to cry."

Her simple observation elicited a rush of emotion. My heart squeezed, and tears wicked up through the tightness. I took another swallow of coffee and a deep breath. Although I didn't know Soraya all that well, I trusted her, and I really could use someone to talk to.

With her warm gaze regarding me, the full tale of my fling with Ryan came tumbling out. "You can see where I messed up. I let myself get hopeful when that was a dumb idea. Honestly, I didn't even let myself get hopeful, it's just that I know I was at risk of being stupid. So, I got smart. Ryan isn't making it easy to move on. I saw him on my walk over, and that's what made me almost cry," I finished.

Soraya's gaze was considering as she took a slow sip of her tea. Cocking her head to the side, she said, "Not many people know Ryan very well."

"I can see that," I said slowly, not sure where she was going with this.

"He takes a business approach to dating." She shook her head slightly and pursed her lips. "If there is such a thing."

"I think there is, but I don't do business dating. My father was an asshole. He was a lot like Ryan. I'm not saying Ryan's an asshole. But my father was wealthy. He had a fling with my mother. Unfortunately for all of us, she got pregnant."

Soraya gave me a pointed look. "It is most certainly *not* unfortunate. The world is lucky to have you."

I smiled. "I didn't mean it like that. I'm blessed. My mother's a wonderful woman, and her whole family is amazing. But my father was never around. He never wanted anything more than a fling. She pined after him for years and so did I. I promised myself I would never do that. Not to myself."

Our food arrived. After we had started eating, Soraya looked over again. "That's heartbreaking, but that doesn't mean that's what will happen. Ryan might be wealthy, but he's not an asshole. Until you, I would've said he didn't want anything serious. He's secretly a softie. Hardly anyone knows how close he and his brother were. You know he's on the board of that animal shelter program, right?"

At my nod, Soraya continued, "Do you know how he ended up on the board?" She didn't wait for my reply. "His brother was on the board before he died. Ryan is on that board because he's purely sentimental. He loved his brother, and they both loved dogs. I'm not going to pretend I'm best friends with Ryan. I only know him through his friendship with Graham. They grew apart during college, then life got in the way, but he's one of the few people Graham totally trusts. I won't get off on a long tangent, but Graham has his own baggage when it comes to friends. It's a big deal for Graham to trust someone. Ryan has an easy out if you don't matter to him. You gave it to him. My guess is you really mean something to him. Plus, it's obvious he means something to you. If you could see your face when you talk about him, you'd know what I mean."

My heart gave an achy thump, and I wanted to cry again, but I was *not* going to cry over Ryan in a coffee shop. I took a sip of coffee and breathed my way through it.

Soraya let the topic of Ryan drop after that. By the time we were leaving, she'd determined it was best for her to make a personal introduction to the tattoo artist she'd recommended for me.

"Here we are," Soraya said, gesturing to a sign ahead, Tig's Tattoo and Piercing.

She tugged me inside. A man looked up from where he was seated on a stool. The man stood, a quick smile flashing across his face when he saw Soraya. "Hey, what brings you here?"

Soraya looked from me to him and back with a smile. "This is my friend, Adelaide. Isn't her name beautiful?"

The man inclined his head with a nod. "I'm Tig. Nice to meet you." His gaze returned to Soraya. "Of course, her name is beautiful."

"Just call me Addie," I added.

"Addie needs a tattoo repaired," Soraya

explained. "I told her you were the best, and you're my friend, so you better do it right."

Tig rolled his eyes. "I think it's Addie's decision." His eyes shifted to me.

"If Soraya trusts you, then I do too."

"Okay, let's take a look."

I shrugged out of my down jacket, which Soraya promptly took from me and folded over her elbow. "Right here," I said turning my hand to the side so he could see the scars. The pink had started to fade.

"I see. Went right through that vine. How'd you hurt yourself?" he asked as I lowered my arm.

"She was trying to break into Ryan Blake's basement," Soraya said, unable to keep from laughing.

Tig's brows hitched up. "Breaking and entering. That's a story."

"I'm not a criminal," I said with a sigh. "My dog got into his basement. Apparently, through his neighbor's broken basement door, not his. I heard my dog barking."

Tig chuckled. "Those scars are pretty fresh, so we'll need to wait until the area is completely healed. When the pink fades, it'll be ready. In the meantime, think about what you want done. I can just fill in where the vine is broken, or we could add a flower to match what you already have."

"What kind of flowers are those anyway?" Soraya asked.

"Jasmine flowers. My favorite."

"What do they mean?" she asked next.

"They're often associated with love," I explained.

Soraya's brows hitched up. "Oh, well, isn't that interesting?"

I wasn't ready to wonder why she made that comment, so I looked back at Tig. "Do I need to call to schedule?"

"Unless you decide on something big, I can fit you in. Soraya can give you my number. Just call the day before you want to stop by."

Moments later, Soraya and I were back out on the sidewalk. She cast me a satisfied smile. "Tig will take care of you, and it'll look great. Unless you want to keep the scar as a souvenir," she teased.

Glancing over, I rolled my eyes. "The scars will be a souvenir no matter what because I only want to fix the part where the vine's broken."

"So, are you going to give Ryan a chance?" Her gaze sobered as she asked me. Much as she tended to be outspoken, I sensed she sincerely cared about how things went for Ryan and me.

I took a breath and let it out. "I don't know. I'm pretty sure the whole concept of opposites attract isn't going to be that helpful for us."

Soraya stopped on the sidewalk at a red light as the hum of traffic carried on around us with its background cacophony. "Ryan can seem like an uptight asshole. Trust me, I've seen how he operates. But he likes you. Like he *really* likes you."

"But how do you know? Has Graham mentioned something to you?"

Soraya chuckled. "Not particularly. He did say after we met you at the charity ball that it was obvious Ryan really liked you, but for me, it's just a gut feeling. Ryan is prone to being sarcastic, and he can be a total dick. It's a miracle he didn't call the police on you that night he found you. That pretty much said it all for me."

I rubbed the edge of my sleeve with my thumb and finger, the silky outer surface of my down jacket slippery under my fingertips. "Well, we'll see."

Soraya narrowed her eyes. "That's all I get?"

"I don't know. Just because you're madly

in love and overwhelmed with pregnancy hormones doesn't mean the rest of us are."

Soraya rolled her eyes and nudged me with her elbow. "I think my pregnancy hormones might be onto something."

———

The following day, I stopped by to visit Trixie, and ended up spilling the whole story about Ryan all over again. Because, yeah, my heart just wouldn't shut up. I was also way too curious to know more about Ryan, to piece together the puzzle of his heart.

"What happened to his brother?" I asked, wanting more than the sketch of details I had.

"Colin was diagnosed with Ewing's sarcoma. The family had the best health insurance money could buy, but it didn't matter. He died five years ago when he was twenty-eight. He was only a year older than Ryan." Trixie closed her eyes for a moment. Her expression was pained when she opened them again. "Men don't show emotion often. I knew Colin from our work on the board together, so I went to the funeral. Ryan was utterly devastated. He didn't shed a tear in public, but his grief was plain to see. Things only got worse between Ryan and his father after that. Colin had served as a buffer between the two of them. After he died, they stopped talking."

"That's so sad," I breathed.

"It is. Life can be sad and unfair. But you carry on anyway. Don't let yourself be fooled about Ryan. If my hunch is right, you've won the best of him."

My whopping total of two new friends appeared to be in agreement on the subject of Ryan.

Trixie gave me a long look as I stood from her kitchen table to leave. "I only have one more thing to say."

"What's that?" I asked.

"When you get old like me, there are a few lessons you learn very well. The more regrets you have, the more time you have to think about those regrets when you grow older. Try to keep the balance in your bank of regret low. Because it's money you can never spend."

Chapter Thirty-Three

ADDIE

The following day, I headed to the appliance store again, this time to select my new oven. Everything Trixie said yesterday about Ryan kept spinning through my mind. I wanted to talk to him, but I needed to gather my thoughts into something sensible first.

Trixie's comments about regret had also pierced me. If her hunch about Ryan and me was right, I might regret not giving him a chance for the rest of my life.

When I stepped into the appliance store again, I walked by the refrigerator section, and a memory slammed into me. It wasn't as if my encounter with Ryan here before had been romantic. Yet, it felt like it now. He'd patiently helped me and even made sure my new refrigerator was all properly installed before he left.

You're an emotional wreck. You're about to start crying in the middle of an appliance shop over a man. Now would be the time to get your shit together, Addie.

I mentally swore at my critical voice. I couldn't stop myself from slipping my phone out of my purse and pulling up Ryan's last text.

Addie, I'm hoping we can talk. Please.

He'd sent that text four days ago. I'd never replied. A twinge of guilt stung my heart. Despite my fears, I knew I would regret it if I didn't at least talk to Ryan.

Before I could chicken out again and before my doubts could run roughshod over my hope, I typed out a quick reply.

Let's talk.

As I was returning my phone to my purse, it vibrated again. Turning it over in my hand, I saw Ryan's reply.

Where are you?

I tried to ignore that sense of hope beating on the door to the closet where I'd locked it in my heart. I was going to be reasonable and rational about this.

I'm back at the appliance store getting a new oven. Maybe we can meet for dinner?

6?

Sounds good. Where should I meet you?

My heart was making a racket inside my chest, and I was smiling like a foolish girl in the middle of a freaking appliance store. All over a man I knew I needed to be careful with even if I decided to give us a chance.

I'll find you.

??

Ryan's replay was confusing. When he didn't respond again quickly, I shrugged to myself and put my phone away. I was here for a reason, and it certainly wasn't to stand there and stare at my phone wondering when Ryan might explain his nonsensical answer.

I headed to the oven section. Just like with the refrigerator, I felt utterly lost with all of the options and wondered if I should just get the same brand as I had for my refrigerator. Surely, if Ryan thought that was a good brand, they probably made good ovens too. Right?

As I was leaning forward to look inside one of the models on the floor, the hairs on the back of my neck stood, and I knew Ryan was there. I straightened, closing the oven slowly, and turned around to find him approaching.

My heart galloped like a horse at the start

of a race, and I soaked in the sight of him. Sweet baby Jesus. It just was *not* fair for him to be so handsome. His dark hair was rumpled as if he'd run a hand through it a few too many times. He walked with easy confidence, and my eyes ate up the way he filled out his suit.

He stopped right in front of me, and I curled my hand more tightly around the handle on the oven door. I needed something to help hold me up.

"Is this what you meant when you said you'd find me?"

Ryan nodded, a smile teasing at the corners of his lips.

"Are we not having dinner?"

"I was hoping I could have the whole afternoon with you and then dinner."

My eyes widened, and my heart kept on running its race.

"I have a lot to say," he offered, his eyes searching my face.

"Oh?"

I felt as if I were flailing around inside. Trixie's comments had nudged my guard back down, and I couldn't quite manage to keep up my steely distance.

Ryan closed the distance between us, maybe all of three feet. He looked downright

delicious in his suit. It was navy and deep-
ened the blue of his glacial eyes. He looked
tired, and my heart squeezed.

"Here's the thing," he began, "I think I
love you. I know you probably have a long list
of reasons why it might not be worth giving
me a chance, but I thought maybe you could
give me a chance to convince you it's
worth it."

My heart felt as if it tripped and fell. That
was me, stumbling and falling like a foolish
girl. He thought he loved me?

I swallowed and tried to quell the clamor
of joy with its little footsteps pounding as it
broke down the door inside my heart.
"What?"

Oh wow, I was so *not* cool, calm, and
collected.

"I love you." His words came out
stronger this time, the unguarded look in his
eyes nearly undoing me and weakening my
knees.

Ryan erased what little distance was left
between us and wrapped me in his arms. I
could feel the beat of his heart against my ear
when I tucked my head into the crock of his
neck.

He leaned his head beside mine, and I
could feel his eyelashes brush against my

cheek. "I thought you said you *think* you love me," I murmured.

Hooray for me. I managed to string more than one word together.

"Well, I've never been in love, so I wasn't totally sure. If it means I think about you whenever you're not with me, and I worry about you all the time, and I miss you so much it hurts, well then, I'm pretty sure that might be love. Or so I hear."

Leaning my head back, I watched as Ryan's eyes opened, those dark lashes nearly curling to touch his cheeks. "Oh God, if I'm going to be in love with you, I have to deal with how ridiculously handsome you are."

Ryan's mouth hitched up at one corner. It felt as if his gaze was a physical caress, and little earthquakes followed every resounding beat of my heart. It was all emotion with Ryan, and it terrified me. I didn't feel as if I could control it and corral it to my whims and wishes.

"I suppose I have to point out the obvious," he said, a chuckle rumbling in his chest.

"What's obvious?" My smile was so wide my cheeks almost ached from it.

"In case you missed it, you're quite beautiful. Stunning, really. Trust me when I tell you that when I'm in a room with you, you're the one who stands out.

His words spun streamers around my heart, each one cinching a little tighter than the last. With my heart in my throat, and joy and hope throwing glitter in the air, I stared back at him.

"Come on now. No need to overdo it."

Ryan chuckled again. He brushed my hair away from my cheek. "I'm not trying to flatter you. One of the things I love about you is you don't focus too much on appearances. That's probably why you never noticed just how fucking beautiful you are."

"Oh." I tried to take a breath, but I only got a little sip of air. It was hard to think with the way my heartbeat echoed through my body.

Emotion could be a noisy thing in a body, or so I was discovering. I'd completely forgotten where we were until a voice intruded. "Excuse me, can I help you?"

Looking to my side, I found a rather cheerful store employee. She had a broad smile on her face and was looking curiously between Ryan and me.

"Oh, um," I began, giving my head a shake because I was too flustered to think clearly. "I'm here to get an oven." I looked up at Ryan. "What should I get?"

He held my eyes through several beats of my heart, and heat spread like little licks of fire over my skin.

"Am I interrupting something?" the young woman asked as if that wasn't obvious.

Ryan looked toward her. "You are, but we do need to get an oven. Give us a minute."

"Okay," she chirped, giving us a cheerful wave as she turned and walked briskly over to answer a ringing phone in the circular desk situated in the center of the section.

"Do you trust me to pick out your oven?" he asked.

"Absolutely. I love my refrigerator, and I have all the faith that I'll love whatever oven you pick out. It better be gas or propane though. I like to cook, and I can't deal with an electric stove," I added pointedly.

"Understood. I just need one thing first."

"What?"

"A kiss."

I was smiling when his lips met mine.

Chapter Thirty-Four

RYAN

I considered myself as a man who thought through every contingency. I usually was. Except, apparently, when it came to Addie.

We'd ordered her stove and arranged for it to be delivered. Small problem. I needed her, and I honestly couldn't wait. With my emotions right at the surface, and a desire that ran so deep and so fiercely for her spinning into the current of need rushing through me, well, I was near frantic by the time we got back to her place.

Unfortunately, the delivery guy had texted me to tell me they would be there within twenty minutes. I needed more than twenty minutes. Lots more.

With Addie's hand warm in mind as we

stepped through her front door, I was wrestling hard to slay my lust for her into some sort of submission.

The sound of the door shutting behind us when Addie closed it was like the lash of a whip in the air. I was attuned to every one of my senses, all of them hyper-aware and focused on Addie. Each sensation, no matter how mundane or unrelated to her, fed into my need.

When she turned to look at me, I let myself absorb the sight of her. Her dark hair was windblown and messy. The little tiny freckles on her skin drew me closer. I needed to count them all some day.

She had little freckles scattered over her body. They were the constellations that mapped her secrets, or so I thought in my heady desire and lust.

Her cheeks were tinged with pink. She slipped out of her down jacket and hung it on the coat rack by the door. She was wearing another one of those silky blouses she seemed to have a penchant for. All I could think was I needed to unbutton it. A black fitted wool skirt covered her purple tights, and she wore those cowboy boots she seemed to love to pieces.

Before I even thought it through—because, let's face it, I never thought anything through with Addie—I was stepping closer to her.

She squeaked. "Ryan! What are you doing?"

"I need you," I said as I looked deep into her eyes. "Now."

She didn't say anything, but I knew she understood. She lifted her hand to cup my cheek, drawing my face down towards hers. Our lips brushed together, and the electricity spun around us.

The next few moments were a blur. I tore her blouse open, and my lips pressed hot, open mouthed kisses along her jaw and down her neck. I dampened the silk of her bra over her nipples and yanked her skirt up around her hips as I lifted her against me and pressed her back against the door.

She shoved my shirt up as she unzipped my fly and curled her palm around my achingly hard arousal. Even with Addie, I didn't think I'd ever been so driven that I tore her clothes. This time I did, yanking at her tights until I heard the fabric tear and found the damp silk between her thighs. I groaned against her skin where my lips were pressed at the base of her throat when I pushed the silk out of the way and found her dripping wet core.

"Need to be inside you," I rasped as I lifted my head. Her eyes were dark, reflecting the fierce, burning need I felt inside.

"Hurry," she gasped.

In a fumbled rush, she shoved my slacks down just far enough that my cock bounced free. Gripping it in my palm, I didn't even wait. The moment I felt her slick desire against my cockhead, I surged deeply, filling her instantly. She let out a rough cry, followed by a satisfied little hum. Her channel pulsed and rippled around me, a tight sheath.

I managed one breath before I drew back and sank inside her again. I couldn't make it slow, but Addie certainly didn't make it easy. With her legs curling around me, she arched into every pounding stroke I made into her. The little noises at the back of her throat pushed me faster and faster. The door rattled behind us while I fucked her roughly against it.

For a second, I thought I was going to lose control before she came. With no finesse whatsoever, I reached between us, pressing my thumb over her clit as I stroked into her and filled her once more.

She cried out sharply, and the sound

echoed in the entryway. My release slammed through me so hard I was relieved I had the door to help me keep my balance. My palm slapped against it while I shuddered, and my release poured into her.

My head fell to the sweet curve of her neck as my breath came in ragged heaves. She smelled so good, like sugar and vanilla. The emotion was cresting inside of me, and I scrambled to gather myself as my release subsided.

When I finally lifted my head, Addie opened her eyes slowly from where her head had fallen back against the door. Through her heavy-lidded gaze, she smiled softly.

"I missed you."

Joy, such an unfamiliar feeling for me, gave a little jump in my heart, almost like a startled animal. "I missed you so fucking much."

At that moment, I felt the vibration of my phone in my pocket and its chime rang out in the entryway.

"Fuck. I'm guessing that's the alert I asked for."

"Alert?"

"Yeah. When I spoke to the delivery guy, I asked him to send an alert when they were within five minutes. We should maybe get dressed."

Addie giggled, and the sound cinched around my heart, the feeling so sweet I didn't even know what to think of it. "We never really undressed."

Leaning forward, I pressed my lips to hers once more. "Not quite."

After I reluctantly untangled myself from Addie and began to pull my clothes back together, I glanced over at her while she buttoned her blouse, a most unfortunate circumstance. I could use plenty of Addie disheveled and half-dressed because she was so damn sexy. "Where's Barnable?"

"He's with Trixie. She said she could keep him for a few hours while I took care of my appliance shopping. You can walk with me to get him. She'll be excited to see us."

"She will?"

Addie shimmied her hips as she tugged her skirt down over her torn tights. She smiled sheepishly when she looked back at me. "Yeah. I had a little talk with her yesterday. She gave me some advice about regret. Also, if you didn't know it, she thinks you're the bee's knees."

We put ourselves back together, just in time for the doorbell minutes later.

———

After Addie's oven was installed that evening, I took her out for dinner just as I'd planned. While we waited for our food to arrive, I enjoyed the sight of Addie. She'd put her hair up in some kind of complicated knot with loose tendrils dangling to frame her face. With silver hoop earrings that swung when she moved, I wanted to lean over and press kisses down the slender column of her neck.

She looked over at me. "What?" I said when I saw the somber look in her eyes.

"Oh, did I tell you I found someone to fix this?" she asked, lifting her hand.

My eyes caught on her wrist. "Oh right. Soraya mentioned something about that."

"From when I tried to break in," she said with a sly grin. "See, I'll get a flower over the broken spot." She slid her hand across the table. I studied the jagged line left behind by the scar that broke the winding vine around her wrist.

Lifting my hand, I traced my finger over the scars. "You can't forget me even if you want to," I teased.

"I couldn't," she said, her voice husky and solemn.

My heart kicked up a few notches.

As I was basking in the moment, we were interrupted by Marla. Of all people. I hadn't seen her come in the restaurant, so I didn't know if she was alone or not. She stopped by our table, glancing between us before her eyes settled on mine.

The look in her gaze was cold and annoyed. "Well, hello, Ryan," Marla said sharply.

For a second, I was beyond annoyed, but I decided to simply be honest. "Hello, Marla. I need to apologize."

Addie looked puzzled, but I hoped she would wait for a minute.

Marla's eyes widened. "Oh? Whatever for?" Marla was nothing if not polite.

I gestured towards Addie, reaching for Addie's hand where it sat on the table and giving it a squeeze as I brushed my thumb back and forth across her knuckles. "This is Addie." It was clear Marla was confused, but she cast a tight smile in Addie's direction before looking back to me. "I need to apologize because I lied to you on the phone the last time we spoke."

"You did?"

"I did. It's not that I don't do romance, or that I'm not interested in marriage. It's that I'm in love with Addie." I looked at Addie when I spoke. My heart lurched in my chest when I heard the soft gasp from her lips, and her fingers tightened in mine.

I looked back toward Marla. I was prepared to see anger in her eyes, but her expression was bemused. "Wow, Ryan Blake, the eternal bachelor, has finally fallen." She smiled wistfully and glanced toward Addie. "I'm happy for both of you. Love is a rare thing indeed. With the way you two look at each other, you might want to be careful in public." Her eyes were laughing when she looked back in my direction. "Good for you, Ryan. I always knew you were a good man." With that, she inclined her head.

"I hope you find the same," I added just before she turned away.

Marla shrugged. "Thank you. I'll hope for the best."

After she departed, I looked back toward Addie. "Really? You love me?"

"Absolutely. I already told you earlier. I'm kind of an idiot. To sum it up, you can thank Graham Morgan and Ask Ida for knocking some sense into me."

Addie grinned. "I'll do that." She paused, her eyes searching mine as her grin faded. "I need to explain something," she began.

"You don't have to explain anything."

"I need to for me. Obviously, my dad passing away brought some things up. The thing was, he was never there for me in any way other than his bank account. Don't get me wrong, I never went without, and for that, I'll always be grateful. But my mother spent years wishing for more. He was just a rich businessman who never intended to be serious, much less have a child. I was truly an accident. My mother eventually came to her senses, but I promised myself I would never be stupid like that. Although I know you're nothing like my father now that I know you, on the surface, there were some similarities. Then, I heard that phone call..." She shrugged, her cheeks turning pink. "If I didn't care so much, it wouldn't have mattered. I was already afraid I was falling for you, and I kind of panicked."

A sense of trepidation slipped through my heart, an icy breeze elicited by any thought of my own father. Or rather, the man who raised me. But this was Addie, and I wasn't going to be afraid. If she could be honest, so could I.

"I get it, and you certainly don't need to apologize. I should explain something too. I've told you a bit about my father. I promised myself I would never let anyone experience the kind of life I had growing up.

He and my mother had an absolutely awful marriage. Although she wasn't as awful as he was, she buried herself in alcohol and misery. I was afraid somehow I would become him, and I didn't want to put anyone through that." Addie squeezed my hand, the warmth in her gaze a balm to the old wounds left behind. "I'm okay now, but something I haven't had a chance to tell you about helped me a little bit. When my brother died, he arranged for genetic testing on both of us through an attorney. He set it up so it wouldn't happen until five years after he died. Lord knows why he chose that time frame, but he did. Long story short, I learned not long after I met you that the man we thought was our father wasn't. It was freeing to learn I don't share his genetics. I know that's not all that makes a person who they are, but for some reason it mattered to me."

Addie and I stared at each other. It felt as if an arc of electricity bounced between our hearts. Our stories were different, but we both were who we were in spite of the fathers we had. Perhaps that would only bind us tighter together in the future. And I knew we had a future. One in which I never intended to let her go.

"You are anything but a cold, miserable

man, Ryan Blake. I knew that the moment I saw you with Barnable," Addie said earnestly.

"So, you fell for me because of your dog?"

"Well, that and the sex. But my dog is a deal-breaker."

EPILOGUE

Addie

Approximately two years later

"No," I said, trying to inject as much firmness as I could into that single word.

Ryan began to say something, but I cut in immediately. "This is getting absolutely ridiculous. I'm only six months pregnant, and I'm *fine*. I just want to take Barnable for a walk. I'm not going to be alone. Soraya is meeting me, and don't you dare leave the office to meet us there."

I was pretty sure Ryan made the insides of his cheeks bleed to keep from arguing, but he acquiesced. I got off the phone after assuring him I'd call once I was back home.

Only moments later, I met Soraya in the park.

"He what?" Soraya exclaimed, coming to a stop on the sidewalk where we were walking Barnable.

"Ridiculous, right?" I asked.

"Jesus. I didn't think it was possible, but Ryan might be worse than Graham was when I was pregnant."

"He's driving me insane. I love him, but I have to get out of the house. Thank God he has to leave for work five days a week. I can't have him with me all the time because he hovers like crazy."

Surprising me, Ryan had suggested we move into my place after we got married. I'd been gradually working my way through updating Aunt Eleanor's home, but there'd been a lot of work to do. Ryan had explained he had no attachment to his family's place and preferred to move on. With his help, we'd done a major overhaul of what was now *our* home while we stayed temporarily at his place. Everything was updated and decorated with my eye, so it was much warmer and welcoming than the home where Ryan had grown up. Although I'd never met his parents, it was as if he shook off the last of his painful childhood when he moved out.

All of that was great, except he was *still* driving me batshit crazy ever since I'd gotten pregnant.

Soraya grinned and rolled her eyes. "Not that I had any doubts before this, but they do say the great ones fall the farthest." She slipped her hand through my elbow. "Here, I'll keep you steady," she teased as we began walking again.

Barnable trotted along on my other side. I unconsciously rubbed my palm over my round belly.

Soraya kept talking. "I can't wait to tell Graham. He loves to give Ryan hell. Of course, he drove me just as crazy as Ryan's driving you. Nothing's worse than an obnoxiously overprotective man trying to protect you from something he can't really do anything about."

"So true."

Soraya and I had become closer over the last two years. Ryan used to work so much, he rarely found time to be social with anyone. That did *not* work for me. I needed time with friends, so by extension, he had more time with friends as well.

After Soraya delivered me back home, I walked in to find Ryan unexpectedly home. "What are you doing here?" I asked. He'd been at the office for some meetings when he called earlier.

"You didn't answer my text," he said as if that was perfectly obvious.

"Babe, I didn't realize you had texted," I said, fumbling in my pocket to pull my phone out and see five texts from him in the last half hour.

I narrowed my eyes and rested a hand on my hip, although I couldn't help the little spin of joy that buzzed through me. Much as I enjoyed being an independent woman, I didn't mind Ryan loving me to the point of annoyance. "You were freaking out because I was taking a walk? Ryan, we've got three months left in this pregnancy."

The annoyance and downright fear in his expression faded. He stepped closer, catching my hand in his and reeling me to him. "I'm not handling this very well."

"Ya think?" I teased.

Ryan smoothed his hand over my belly. "I don't think, I know. I can't bear it if anything happens to you and the baby."

"We're fine," I said, leaning up and pressing a kiss on the side of his jaw. "Also, could we please have sex?"

Although I had physically dragged Ryan to my doctor's appointment with me solely for the purpose of her explaining to him that it was perfectly safe for us to have sex, he was still being difficult.

He leaned his forehead against mine. "If you insist."

———

RYAN

Another six months later

"Ryan?" Graham's voice nudged me.

I hadn't even realized my eyes had fallen closed until I dragged them open.

Graham chuckled softly. "Up with the baby last night?" he asked, his tone dry.

"How'd you guess?" I muttered as I gave my head a shake and reached for the cup of coffee that was permanently on the side of my desk these days. I thanked God for Hazel daily because she stayed on top of making sure I had fresh coffee at all times.

"I've done baby duty. You learn to function without sleep after a while. I don't hear you complaining much, though."

Graham had stopped by to grab lunch while we chatted about various business matters. I met his gaze and shrugged, my lips curling in a smile automatically. "There's nothing to complain about."

"Told ya it would be worth it," Graham said with satisfaction.

I laughed and took a long swallow of my coffee. "You can tell me you were right as many times as you'd like. I completely agree."

That evening, I looked across the kitchen table at Addie. I was certain she was going to keep getting more beautiful to me. Her dark hair was pulled up in a messy bun with a few loose tendrils hanging around her face and a portion of it falling out completely in the back. She'd explained Colin, our son, had yanked it out earlier when she was feeding him.

Addie set her fork down and pushed her plate away, lifting her eyes to meet mine. "Do you think he'll stay asleep?" she whispered.

"I hope so," I whispered in return. "Why are we whispering?"

Addie giggled, and the sound spun through the air, cinching like a lasso around my heart. Addie had well and truly captured my heart for good going on two years now. I fell deeper in love with her every time she giggled.

"Because Colin's asleep, and I don't want to wake him up."

I stood from the table, rounding to her side. Without a word, I caught her hands in mine and tugged her up. Considering that to get to our bedroom, we had to walk past Colin's bedroom, that wasn't happening.

If there was one thing Addie and I absolutely didn't care about, it was where we made love. I lifted her hips onto the kitchen counter, resting my hands on either side. "I missed you," I murmured as I pressed one kiss and then another on each corner of her mouth.

"I'm right here," she said, her eyes glinting.

"I meant while I was at work today. I fell asleep when Graham stopped by with some takeout for lunch."

Addie lifted her hand, trailing her fingertips along the stubble on my jaw." I love you, Ryan Blake," she said, her tone going solemn quickly.

"I love you too." Those words came easy for me now. Addie made them easy.

"Was it worth it then?" she asked.

"Was what worth it?"

"Catching me almost breaking into your basement."

"So worth it." I leaned forward and caught her lips in a quick kiss, even slipping in some tongue.

Drawing back, I added, "However, I still dispute the "almost" part of that sentence. You were totally breaking in."

Addie angled her head to the side, a teasing smile stretching across her face. "I never set foot in your house until you invited me in."

With that, she yanked at my clothes and made me forget everything for the next few minutes.

I didn't even mind that, only seconds after I found my release inside of her, the baby monitor crackled to life with Colin's cry.

That was the thing. When you fell in love, everything was okay. Life was perfect with Addie. She was everything I didn't expect, and she was *everything* to me.

———

Want to keep up with all of the new releases in Vi Keeland and Penelope Ward's Cocky Hero Club world? Make sure you sign up for the official Cocky Hero Club newsletter for all the latest on our upcoming books:

https://www.subscribepage.com/CockyHeroClub

Check out other books in the Cocky Hero Club series:
http://www.cockyheroclub.com

ACKNOWLEDGMENTS

Gracious thanks to Vi Keeland & Penelope Ward for inviting me to participate in this project, and to the team at Cocky Hero Club for such wonderful support in the process.

Thank you to my editor for helping me make Ryan & Addie's story the best it could be. To Terri D. for her eagle eyes.

To my husband who balances me in so many ways. Last and never least, to my dogs who are there for every story.

xoxo
   J.H. Croix

ABOUT THE AUTHOR

USA Today Bestselling Author J. H. Croix lives in a small town in the historical farmlands of Maine with her husband and two spoiled dogs. Croix writes contemporary romance with sassy women and alpha men who aren't afraid to show some emotion. Her love for quirky and relatable characters shines through in her writing. Take a walk on the wild side of romance with her bestselling novels!

Places you can find me & my books:

https://jhcroixauthor.com/books/
https://jhcroixauthor.com
jhcroix@jhcroix.com

Sign up for my newsletter for information on new releases & get a FREE copy of one of my books!

http://jhcroixauthor.com/subscribe/

facebook.com/jhcroix

instagram.com/jhcroix

bookbub.com/authors/j-h-croix

www.ingramcontent.com/pod-product-compliance
Lightning Source LLC
Chambersburg PA
CBHW030012200726
48284CB00016B/272